Matt stopped. H  beats. "What are you c　　ｇ

The darkest parts of me, those that I kept stuffed way down inside, surged to the surface. My face burned with indignation. I was Kate the Shrew at her best.

"How dare you! You and your pretty little Live Like King Tut fable. You kiss me and tell me you liked it. You say you are my biggest fan. You pretend to bare your soul. You think I can't figure out what's going on? All you want is for me to believe that you're a good guy, so you can leave me hanging out for a pack of wolves. So I can end up as dead as Mariella. Well, damn you all to hell!"

Slick as spit, Matt reached out and took my hands. "It's not like that."

I wrenched away. "Keep away from me, you—you Judas!"

Praise for Roxanne Dunn

MURDER UNREHEARSED was a finalist in the Pacific
Northwest Writer's Association (PNWA) contest.

Murder Unrehearsed

by

Roxanne Dunn

Murder Unrehearsed

Cover Art by *Kim Mendoza*

The Wild Rose Press, Inc.
PO Box 708
Adams Basin, NY 14410-0708
Visit us at www.thewildrosepress.com

Publishing History
First Mainstream Mystery Edition, 2020
Trade Paperback ISBN 978-1-5092-3268-0
Digital ISBN 978-1-5092-3269-7

Published in the United States of America

Dedication

In memory of my mother,
Emma Charlotte Rosenkranz Gloer,
who taught me to keep trying

Chapter One

I used to swear that nothing ever happened at Lake Sterling. So far, nothing had. I pressed the accelerator, and without any serious mechanical noises, my faithful little old car, Bogey, tackled the winding, paved-but-still-potholed upgrade in Washington State's Cascade Mountains. My dog, Bear, an Akita, perched on the bucket seat beside me. He narrowed his eyes to slits and let the wind blow from the open convertible onto his handsome face. I grabbed a handful of fur at the base of his neck and felt its texture—tough, strong, reassuring.

"Why can't there be a man with your good qualities?"

Just like a man, he said nothing.

I crested the hill and glimpsed the cold, deep, steep-sided lake below, shimmering in the light of a crescent moon. Above me stretched the Milky Way, bright and star-packed. After a few minutes the headlights flashed on "The Sheltons" and we turned into our driveway. I liked the freshly painted sign. It said I belonged, told me I had roots here, and brought back memories of languid, growing-up summers. I'd arrived at the perfect hideaway, our family cabin, surrounded by forest and perched on a rocky hillside overlooking a small, secluded cove.

As the tires crunched on gravel, I coasted down the slope and turned into the carport.

"Just wait 'til Grandma Garnet hears about this," I told Bear.

My grandmother, diminutive, white-haired Garnet Elizabeth Anne Windsor, who wore her pearls every day, and traced her family back to England's King Edward IV, feared nothing. I loved her to pieces and she loved me right back. That didn't stop her from pointing out the uncomfortable truth that whenever I got hurt or scared, I fled.

"That, my darling," she always said, "is not the way to live."

And here I was, fleeing again. All because Alex St. John said he'd grab some Thai takeout and help me prepare for auditions. No matter how much I wanted the lead role in *Taming of the Shrew*, at Viva!, Seattle's little repertory theater in the Fremont neighborhood, I wasn't going to fall for that line again. I didn't even think about it. I threw the script into my duffel, added my toothbrush and pajamas, and headed for the cabin. He had broken my heart once, and I wasn't about to give him another chance. As I got out of the car, I shoved Alex to the back of my mind.

I unlocked the back door and stepped inside. A wave of hot, stuffy air engulfed me. I walked through the kitchen and past the eating bar into the living area. On my right, the lamp that came on when it got dark shone on the big, round, polished, oak table. Off to the left, the comfy leather sofa and cushy old chairs hunkered in the shadows. I opened the sliding glass doors to the deck and pushed aside the wooden shutters. As a cool, sweet breeze filled the cabin, I turned on lights and removed dust covers.

My heartbeat slowed to an easy rhythm that echoed

all the way back to my childhood, to the time when my sister, Harmony, was still alive. At the far end of the living room, I paused beside the fireplace and gazed at the last photo we had of the whole family, taken nearly fourteen years ago, only a few days before she died. I was eight, tall, blue-eyed, and blonde, like Dad and my brother. My sister was five, petite and dark like Mom. Frozen in time, forever five years old. I still missed her small, warm hand in mine.

Bear nudged his dish, reminding me he needed water. As I filled it, I warbled my best imitation of Patsy Cline. I pulled a mattress off the bunk in the back bedroom and dragged it out onto the deck. I put the binoculars beside it in case the yodel call of a loon awakened me in the morning.

In three days, I'd head back over the mountains to Seattle, ready to try out for the role of Kate. I wouldn't think about the last time I auditioned for a major part. Never again would I be rooted to the stage, my mouth opening and closing like a just-caught trout. This time, my performance would be stunning. This time, I'd win the prize.

I'd work with that wretched Alex St. John again, and God help me, this time my heart would not flutter and my knees would not wobble. Not when he looked at me. Not even when he touched me. My name would be on the marquee beside his, and from now on, our romance would exist only on stage.

Okay, I got scared and ran away. But I'd done the right thing. I was so pleased with myself that I ignored Bear's restless sniffing and pacing. I should have paid attention. But I nestled into my sleeping bag, loving the soft warmth against the crisp night air, and laid my head on my old feather pillow. The timeless constellations spread their glory over me and I felt totally secure.

****

Bear's growl vibrated deep in his chest. I rolled onto my side and pulled my sleeping bag over my ear. His furry black chest rumbled again. Hearing the roar of a boat's motor, I sat up and opened my eyes just enough to see the hills on the far side of the lake, purple-gray cutouts pasted against a pale, predawn sky. Fifty feet below the cabin, the water gleamed with the first pink and lavender streaks of light. On the deck, where we lay under the overhanging roof, it was still dark.

The throb of the motor grew louder, then echoed off the cliffs that surround our cove. That meant the boat had come inside our little, U-shaped bay. And the engine was at full throttle. But why would they want to go full speed? Guys often fished around the mouth of the cove, but they trolled, boat barely moving, motor idling, the noise no louder than a mosquito's hum.

I pulled the binoculars out of the case and focused. Bear, satisfied that he'd awakened me, rested his nose on his paws. There was just enough light to see a white runabout cutting through the water, peeling the surface back in long, shining furrows. It was towing a water-skier, a featureless black shape silhouetted against the lake and growing larger every moment. Probably a group of local kids celebrating the end of the school year. Every summer, my older brother and his friends had stayed up all night, then went out skiing just as the sun came up. They'd bragged forever afterward about doing it with bare asses.

Mom never heard that part. Dad always hid his

smile behind his book, and I used to wish I could have been a boy.

The skier was now outside the wake and starting back across. I could almost feel one hand skimming the water, fingers buffeting against the waves. Suddenly, the engine cut out. The skier stretched out the black shadow of his arm and tumbled into the water. The echoes faded. Silence.

Imagining the icy shock, I shivered in sympathy. Later in the day, when the sun beat down blistering hot and the lake took on the appearance of hammered pewter, I'd love the cold, fresh plunge. But in the early twilight, I was happy to leave it to the more foolish, and most likely inebriated, testosterone-filled crowd. I fluffed my pillow.

The engine started up. The roar reverberated off the cliff walls. They had the throttle wide open again. Why? In the middle of the cove, half a city block away, but visible through the lenses of the binoculars, the skier swam toward our dock. A black silhouette against the expanse of shimmering, lavender colored water, he seemed small and fragile. The boat charged toward him, going way too fast. Idiots.

I caught my breath. I remembered the summer when our neighbor's fifteen-year-old nephew was killed by a speeding boat in this cove. "Bear, this is stupid."

The swimmer changed course ninety degrees. The boat veered to follow, rapidly closing. My mouth went dry and my hands started to shake. "Stop," I yelled, getting up onto both knees. They neither slowed nor faltered. "*Stop!*"

I willed them to call off the game. Too late, the guy in the water turned away. The bow struck him hard.

A heavy thud deep in my chest knocked the air out of my lungs. I bit my knuckles to keep from screaming.

Tossing out a huge wake, the boat tilted into a tight circle. A dolphin-like shape bobbed in the water. My chest felt too rigid to breathe. Suddenly afraid that they might see my white pajamas, I dropped to hands and knees and crawled into the cabin. When I looked back over my shoulder, Bear had lifted his head. With its white mask, he'd stand out like a beacon. I signaled him to stay down. He dropped his nose to his paws.

I heard them throttle back, then cut the engine. The echoes died away as I sprinted to the kitchen and grabbed my phone from the counter. It beeped at me. I stared in disbelief at the message "no service." I sprinted back to the open door and watched, hoping it was a practical joke gone tragically awry.

In the stillness, and given the way sound carries over water, I heard a man's voice, masked by waves breaking on shore. "Fuck you . . .slosh . . . slosh . . . chicken shit."

Down on the lake, two black shadows leaned over the side of the boat. One swung a short bat, probably a fish club, up over his head. The club came down. Thunk. Then again. Thunk. Thunk. Like bone breaking. Thunk.

As I crept back to Bear, a second voice, hoarse and urgent, pleaded, "For God's sake, stop."

Thunk. The sound reverberated around the cove. I heard a long, low chuckle, another thunk, then the first man again. "Listen up, fucker . . . slosh, slosh, slosh . . . do to us?"

I squeezed my eyes shut and tried to remember how to say a rosary, as I had been taught in school, but all that came out of my mouth were raspy, asthmatic wheezes.

One of them threw something long and narrow, like a life belt, up over his shoulder into the boat. Then he moved to the helm and started the motor.

My heart pounded as hard as if I had run a fast 10K on a hot day. Stories of people being resuscitated after being underwater bounced in and out of my head. The lake is very cold. I know how to do CPR. Sometimes people go into hibernation. He had to be dead. But what if he wasn't? Would he sink or float? My mind refused to hold a thought long enough to decide. It was like chasing a scrap of paper in the wind.

The boat zoomed away toward the open lake. I bit my lip and forced myself to wait. The wake flattened out, became long lines in the water. They turned up-lake and vanished around the bend. I jumped up and raced across the deck to the stairway leading down to our dock. My bare feet drummed on the wooden treads. Before I reached the first landing, Bear bounded ahead of me. At the bottom, I rushed into the boathouse, fumbled the lines loose from the cleats, threw them into Dad's new super-fast speedboat, and climbed in with Bear beside me. I backed out of the slip, banging against the dock in my haste.

I turned toward the middle of the cove and punched the throttle. The engine sputtered, caught, and I hurtled out, sitting on the edge of the seat. I felt braver talking out loud. "We have to see, Bear. We're the only ones who can help."

I pulled the throttle to idle and zigzagged back and forth, leaned over the side and peered into the water. Nothing. Nothing looked back up at me but my own reflection. "We've got to find him." I stopped the motor and sat on the gunwale, dropped my feet over the side, and slid in.

The frigid water took my breath away. I gasped. Bear stood with his paws on the transom, looking as if he might join me. "Stay," I ordered.

I let out half the air in my lungs and dove. All around me stretched eerie blue-black depths. Nevertheless, I swam and dove several times, hoping to find the water-skier and dreading that I would.

Bear's warm muzzle pressed into my shoulder as I clung to the side of the boat to rest. Although our little bay lingered in the shadow of the hills, the sun had reached the middle of the lake and reflected off the ripples like a million diamonds. It was too late. *I* was too late. I had no hope of finding him.

Hand over hand, I pulled myself around to the back and climbed up over the transom. Under a seat, I found a towel and wrapped it around myself. I wished I had followed them, found out where they went.

I shivered so hard I could barely bring the boat into the boathouse. My fingers had gone numb. I had to look at them to make them cleat the lines.

My legs shook like jelly as I took the long climb up the stairs to the deck.

Clamping my hand onto Bear's collar, I steadied myself against his robust shoulder.

Inside the cabin, I locked the doors and while my mind replayed relentlessly and vividly the sounds and scene, I dried myself and pulled on shorts and a T-shirt.

We rushed out to my car.

I drove three miles to High Haven Marina, gripping the wheel with all my might and watching my mirrors

the whole way.
What if they saw me?

Chapter Two

Surrounded by trees that harbored dense shadows in the undergrowth, the familiar, red-roofed, log-cabin style store at High Haven Marina looked dark, ominous, spooky. No living thing moved. Where the sun touched the far corner of the parking lot, mist spiraled up like remnants of a medieval sacrifice.

I parked as close as I could to the store and got out of the car. I walked without feeling the gravel path under my feet, shivered without sensing the coolness of the air, and saw but could not comprehend the cheerful red and white sign on the door: "CLOSED". I stood there like a wind-up toy that had run down and gaped at it. I had a surreal sensation that I had floated out of my body and was watching from a distance.

Bear nosed me impatiently. I turned to the old-fashioned phone beside the door, kept there as a courtesy to boaters with poor cell reception. I lifted the receiver and watched my shaking fingers punch in the numbers.

"Sheriff." The gravel-filled male voice gave me an anchor in reality.

I let out the breath I'd been holding in. "This is Heather Shelton."

"Harry Shelton's kid?"

Instantly, I felt a lump rise in my throat and swallowed hard. "Yes. Only I'm not a kid anymore. I graduated from UW last year."

He chuckled. "Here I thought I'd come in early and get some paperwork done. This is Jake O'Toole, Heather. I haven't even started the coffee yet. What's got you callin' me at this time of the morning?"

"M-m-murder."

Until I said it, part of me still tried to believe it had been an accident. Admitting it was murder made it hard to breathe. My tongue hardly formed the sounds. My mouth felt as dry as if I had stuffed it with cotton balls, but my story poured out all the same.

The sheriff let the torrent of words rush at him, then said, "Uh-huh."

"He tried to swim away, but the bow hit him hard."

"You sure it was murder?"

My forehead got clammy. I collapsed onto a bundle of firewood stacked beside the phone and leaned my elbows on my knees. "Seriously, they killed him on purpose." I began to cry and my words came out all jerky. "One of them hit him with a club—over and over again."

The sheriff's voice changed to wary. "When exactly did this happen?"

I switched the phone from one shaking hand to the other. "Not more than half an hour ago. It was still mostly dark."

Why hadn't I charged my phone last night? The battery needs at least two bars to connect when I'm at the cabin.

"What happened next?" His voice was still laced with skepticism.

"They left. And . . . I c-c-c-couldn't find him. I tried so hard . . . to find him."

It took me right back to that day when I was eight, when my little sister, Harmony, jumped so hard on the trampoline that she flew right off and landed in the driveway. I tried to help her get up. She didn't move, and even before my mom came to see what was wrong, I knew something terrible had happened. For weeks afterward, I walked around in a daze, both numb and aching. If only I had grabbed her, wrapped my arms around her, and pulled her back down onto the trampoline, I would have kept her safe. Harmony would still be alive.

And Mom wouldn't blame me.

I didn't know the water-skier. He didn't have a face or a name. But I hadn't been able to save him. It made me feel small and achy and hollow again. For several moments, I couldn't speak.

Sheriff O'Toole's tone sharpened. "You still there, Heather?"

I wiped my nose with the hem of my T-shirt. "I couldn't stop them." I bit my lip and tried to stop the tears running down my cheeks. "And I couldn't find him. I dove and dove, but he wasn't there."

"Okay, I'm getting the picture." Resignation tinged his voice. "You alone right now?"

"Bear is here."

I caught my breath. Where was Bear? Panicked, I jumped up and looked around. Where the trail to the lake wound into the forest and disappeared, my dog, tail curling high over his back, poked his nose into the brush, unconcerned.

"*Who's* with you?"

"Bear. My Akita."

"Good. Stick right close to him. You at the cabin?"

12

"I'm at High Haven."

"Anyone else there?"

I pivoted, looked over my shoulder. "No." My heart thudded against my ribs. "God, I hope not."

"I'll be right out." The phone banged in my ear and the line went dead.

Goose bumps stood out on my arms. I climbed into my old car. Bear bounded over, jumped in, and snuffled at my face with his dew-damp muzzle. I drove to a spot where I could keep watch on both the entrance from the road and the path leading from the docks up to the store. With one hand fisted in his neck hair, I tried to calm myself by taking long slow breaths the way I do when I'm standing in the wings waiting for my cue.

"Just wait until Grandma Garnet hears about this," I grumbled to Bear. "How many times has she told me, 'At some point, darling, if you don't stop running away, you will run into something much worse.'"

She was right. I'd run from rehearsing with Alex at the theater and stumbled right onto a stage set for murder.

****

Bear's ears stiffened and he turned his head toward the road. Every muscle in my body tensed. I started the engine, ready to flee. A plain white car appeared between the trees. It drove in and rolled to a stop beside us. The door opened, and a lanky figure in a fresh khaki uniform got out. With thanks to all the good in the universe, I jumped out to meet him.

Jake O'Toole's handshake was the no-nonsense kind. His palm felt dry and callused. His eyes looked right into mine and his mouth didn't smile. I felt him measuring me, looking to see if I had what my dad called character.

"Haven't talked to you since you had railroad tracks on your teeth."

A picture of my first encounter with him flashed into my mind. His hair had been black then. Now it was iron gray, and the frown lines and wrinkles were more deeply etched on his face than they had been, but it was the same cop. Some of the tension eased out of my chest. "You caught Tom, my brother, and Bill Harlan stealing beer out of the creek at the county park."

"You were supposed to be their lookout."

I nodded, surprised that he recalled an incident from ten years ago. I looked at him more carefully— noted the deep grooves that bracketed his mouth, the lively sparkle in his brown eyes, and the lean, alert angles of his body. I did my best to look as if I did indeed have character.

"Tom's gone on to better things by now, I expect. And you? You've stayed clean?"

I felt an I'm-glad-it's-you smile start in my heart and work its way up to my face. I *was* glad. Jake O'Toole reaffirmed the basic goodness of the community. Suddenly, I knew for certain that the murderers had to be outsiders. No one who loved the lake as I did—as he did—would have done something so brutal to another human being.

Jake smiled back, as if to let me know that we were on the same team. He stood still, letting my dog sniff his pant legs. "This critter looks as if he could eat a guy. Probably a good thing he's friendly."

"Tom trains guard dogs, shepherds, mostly, but occasionally Akitas. Bear was a runt, so he gave him to me." Talking about my brother soothed the roiling in

14

my gut. "Runt or not, his jaws are strong enough to break an arm." Bear offered Jake his best silly grin. Some watchdog.

"Hi, buddy." Jake scratched Bear's head. "Now, let's get up to your cabin."

While I banged my door a couple of times to get it to latch, Jake folded his long body into the white sedan. He waited for me to start off, then followed. At the cabin, I stopped by the back door, but he motioned me on into the carport. He drove in and parked beside me. "You leave your car out there, and somebody might drive by and see it and start to wonder if you had a good look at the lake this morning."

I shivered.

Facing our back door, he looked around. "Now, help me remember." He waved a hand toward the right. "It seems to me the Cowans are over there." Then he pointed to the left. "And the Peppers are over there."

"Correct."

"And no one else has a view of this part of the lake," he murmured.

"That's true."

"They around? The Cowans or the Peppers?"

"Neither ever comes over to the lake before the first of July."

"Then most likely, you're the only one who saw this." He pressed his lips together and rocked back onto his heels a couple of times. "Are there footpaths between your places?"

"Only between here and the Cowans. There's a steep ravine between us and Peppers."

"I'll have to check it out."

A cold finger ran down my spine. "Why?" I

15

crossed my arms on my chest and stared up at him. "You think they're here?"

"Not now. Earlier, most likely. They'd check to see if anyone's around. If it was murder."

"I know murder when I see it."

His eyes, set deep under gray-brown thickets, looked as if they could read a person's thoughts, as if they could trap whatever they saw behind their deep brown surface. "Probably."

Even though I had nothing to hide, I felt unsettled. What if he didn't believe me? He had only my word. There was no evidence—absolutely nothing to see.

The water in the cove was extremely deep and very cold, so cold it would take an age for a body to decompose and float to the surface. By then, it could drift out into the lake, even all the way down to the end and into the Quarter Note River. It would take a miracle to find the body. Either the guys in the boat were lucky in their choice of places to kill the water-skier, or they knew a lot about the area.

They had committed the perfect crime—almost. If they had picked any other day in the last month, I wouldn't have been there. I tried to quell the jittery feeling in my chest. I told myself it made sense that they would come to check it out beforehand, to see if anyone was there. But they had no reason to come back.

Jake glanced at the shutters covering the windows. "From back here, it looks closed up. That's good."

The pit of my stomach constricted in a vise. "Look." I gripped Bear's collar more tightly. "Just tell me. Am I in danger?"

"That's a good question."

Chapter Three

Below the cabin, the sapphire water danced, twinkling with millions of beams of light, denying that it concealed a body. I could almost believe it had never happened. Sheriff Jake O'Toole and I stood on the big, wide deck that wrapped the front of the cabin and gazed northward over our cove—three acres of very deep water. I pointed to my favorite rock, over on the west side. It looked like a long, fat cigar standing on end, with a bowler hat on top.

Then I showed him the scraggly pine growing out of a fissure in the cliff on the east. "If you draw a line between those two points and look halfway in between them, that's where he went down, right in the middle."

"We need to talk."

"What do you mean? I've told you everything."

He started across the deck. "You think you have, but that's a far sight away from enough."

"That's all there is." I was talking to three starched creases in the back of his khaki shirt. Oh, and Bear's tail end. "I should never have come over here. I'm going to grab my stuff and head back to Seattle as soon as I lock up."

Jake didn't even glance back over his shoulder. "You're staying. You're a material witness. And you summoned me before breakfast. Got anything to eat up here?"

I whacked my forehead with the palm of my hand. Okay, I hadn't eaten in a long time. I'd make breakfast. Fine. But this was not my fault, and I wasn't staying.

He went down the stairs to the ground and turned in a complete circle, then stood there, looking down. Then he squatted and peered at the feathery green ferns that grew all around the cabin.

I steamed into the kitchen. I had a life, and practicing for auditions was my priority. This was his problem. It was up to him to figure out who did it. We paid cops to catch murderers, didn't we? He just needed to get on it.

Traitor Bear followed Jake while he made a slow circuit of the cabin, and then down the long flight of rough-hewn stairs to the water. While the coffee dripped through the filter, I rummaged in the freezer for Grandma Garnet's cinnamon rolls. The microwave turned them into rich, gooey temptations, and the warm scent of cinnamon reminded me of her kitchen. Grandma Garnet wasn't perfect. Even when I was little, I knew my grandmother was a snob. But she stayed in my room with me all those nights after Harmony died and explained over and over again that it wasn't my fault, no matter what my mother said. I wondered what Grandma would do now.

I marched out onto the deck and yanked the plastic covers off the glass-topped table and a couple of chairs. I was stuffing the covers into the storage bin that doubled as a bench beside the hot tub when I saw Jake and Bear start back up from the lake. As they reached the deck, I grabbed the rolls and carried them out through the sliding door. "Find anything?"

"Not much." He dropped a tiny camera into his

shirt pocket. "A trail of broken ferns along both sides of the cabin and half a dozen nice, clear footprints." He shot a glance at me. "Not your shoe size."

I froze in place. They had been here.

Jake took a step toward me. "Need a hand?"

I stared at him. "When?"

"The footprints? Oh, some time ago. I'd guess last evening."

I remembered what I was doing. I got my feet going again. My hands shook. The pan containing the rolls rattled against the plates.

While I went back for the coffee, Jake held his phone to his ear and paced along the railing, talking to someone named Orlando, clipping his words off short, sounding as if he was in a hurry. "Now I want you to line up two divers pronto, lots of air, and get Sam to pick them up in his boat for me. No dive flags. He should bring his tackle so's to look as if he's merely out fishing. He can troll around and make sure it didn't float ashore. If Sam can't do it, call me back."

Sam Fitzpatrick? The Sam from Sam's Resort? Why him? I didn't get to ask.

The sun, finally high enough to reach over the trees to the deck, glinted off Jake's plain gold wedding band as he came to the table and sat down, still talking. "Right. Right. I've got guys on all the roads already. Had 'em out before you were up, no doubt. Don't worry. No one had time to haul a boat out of the water and get past us." He listened for a moment, and then the patience in his voice changed to exasperation. "Get this, Orlando, we geezers have a few tricks up our sleeves." Pressing his lips together, he tapped the screen and laid the phone beside his plate.

I stifled a grin. "Geezers?" Keeping my gaze on the cinnamon rolls, I handed them to him.

Jake slid his fork under a roll and lifted it high to keep the long, ropey strands of sugar and butter from dripping onto the table. He put it on his plate. "Yeah, well, back in March when the snow started to melt, a body turned up in one of the orchards above Sam's place. Dead several months.

That grabbed my attention. Enough to make me stare at him. "Who? Someone we know?"

"No clues, except it looked like a professional job."

I felt like I'd been punched in the stomach. "Professional? Here? You're kidding."

"Nope."

"Why do you think a professional offed the guy?"

"Can't tell you."

I still couldn't believe it. "You can't tell because you don't know, or you can't tell because it's classified?"

He grinned at me.

I'd always felt safe here. I drummed my fingernails on the table and waited. Surely a professional killer had nothing to do with me.

After a minute, he said, "Anyway, I called for help." Jake took a sip of coffee. A smile tugged at the corners of his lips. "The FBI sent a kid and his almighty bazillion gigabyte computer. Spent two days tapping on those keys, snickering at my old model, and lecturing me on the miracles of modern criminal science."

"And he called you a geezer?"

"Yup. A day or two later, I finally thought of something snappy to say back." Jake shook his head. "But he'd left already."

I was starting to like Sheriff O'Toole. I willed him to borrow a line from an old John Wayne movie, something like, "I'm here now, ma'am. No need to trouble your pretty head further." I pictured the Duke stuffing Grandma Garnet's breakfast roll into his mouth, fortifying himself, and grinning—just like Jake.

I wasn't ready to let things go. *Couldn't* let them go. "Could the murders be related?"

Jake shrugged. "Too soon to know."

"Did the FBI kid and his gigabytes figure out who the bad guy was?"

Jake paused a moment, as if considering. "He had a theory. Then he packed up and left. I admit he had me going, though." His smile started out small, then spread all the way up to his eyes. "I even ordered a new computer the other day." He pushed the pan of rolls in my direction. "I need your help, so you better get your strength up."

I sighed. Apparently, he hadn't taken those old movies to heart.

He worked his way through a gigantic cinnamon roll, cutting off a bite at a time and spearing it with his fork. "Now be quiet. I have to think a bit."

I got up, stalked into the cabin, and packed my duffel. I wished I had paid more attention to the definition of material witness in that criminal behavior class at UW; then I'd know for sure if Jake could make me stay. The more I talked about it, the worse it would be, and it was already bad enough. No matter what, the sound of crunching bones was going to haunt me for a long time. Thinking about that creepy chuckle turned my stomach. It meant the guy bashing the water-skier with the fish club enjoyed it—actually had fun.

If I had to keep going over it in my head, I'd be a wreck: too tired to stay awake, too scared to go to sleep, too tense to focus on my lines. Then almost certainly, I'd bomb the audition next week and the scheming mantrap, Victoria Coronado, would swoop in and grab the role that should be mine. I carried my duffel to the kitchen door, dropped it on the floor. Ready to go.

The problem was, if I left, Grandma Garnet's stiff British soul would not approve. She would see it as a lack of civic responsibility. She would sympathize briefly, but then she'd say, "It's fine to have *une petite* hissy fit, darling, but one must rise above such circumstances."

Okay, okay. I went back to the deck and poured a cup of coffee. Surely it wouldn't take too long to answer Jake's questions. I'd already told him what happened. With luck, he would find the body and arrest the murderers. It would hit the news on TV, and everybody would forget about it after approximately half a day. Then I could block it all out and study my script. I had to. I had to be better than ever. Victoria The Perfect might have snagged my boyfriend with her bright red claws, but she'd win the lead role in *Taming of the Shrew* only if I were in a coma.

Jake slid his plate away. He folded his napkin to its original shape and laid it on the table; took a little spiral note pad out of his shirt pocket and extracted a stubby pencil from the metal coil. "Now. When did you arrive?"

"About one-thirty this morning."

"You came alone?"

"With Bear."

Sheriff O'Toole dropped the pencil and scratched

Bear behind his ears. "With this fierce critter."

I felt a stab of jealousy as my dog leaned into Jake's hand and grinned his silly grin and swished his tail back and forth on the deck.

"Who knows you're here?"

"No one."

He raised both brows in an "Oh, come on" look.

"It's true. I made a spur of the moment decision." This was all Alex's fault.

Jake stared at me for a moment, as if deciding whether I was telling the truth. Then he began, slowly and methodically, to go over every detail from the moment I left Seattle until he met me at High Haven Marina. Whoever made those movies about bungling small town sheriffs hadn't met this one.

O'Toole had a way of turning the questions around and coming back at them from different angles, dredging up details I hadn't even noticed, like the size of the boat, the shape of it, the relative sizes of the two men. The voices. Several times, the ghost of something familiar drifted by, but I couldn't catch it. In the end, in spite of all our efforts, the men in the boat, like the water-skier, had been nothing but featureless silhouettes back-lit by the early morning light on the lake.

After a while, he helped me replace the mattress and sleeping bag on the bunk bed in the bedroom, then inspected the rest of the cabin. "Good," he said, nodding. "It looks as if you just arrived, and by the way, if anyone drops in here, that's what you must tell them. Make sure you tell everyone you drove over this morning."

He glared at me for a moment. "I don't want to hear anything about this anywhere. I'm highly allergic to even a whiff of it on the famous Lake Sterling grapevine."

"Got it." My eyes burned from lack of sleep and my head throbbed. I wanted to go for a run, to burn off the adrenaline that was churning my stomach.

"Now, let's go down to your dock."

I whistled for Bear, five short notes, all the same pitch, all I'd ever mastered, and headed for the stairway that zigzagged down the rocky hillside. By the time I reached the first landing, Bear nudged past me, then bounded down.

At the bottom, Jake strode down the dock. Under the cuffs of his sharply creased khaki pants, I spied the canted heels and pointed toes of cowboy boots. As he moved, they made a hollow echo that bounced up off the water. He ducked his head under the low roof of the boathouse and went in. Bear and I followed. In the cool, dim interior, Jake stood with one hand on his hip, looking down at my father's boat, then jotted a couple of words on his pad.

"What are you writing?"

"There's a towel in the boat and water on the seat. Corroborates your story."

That jolted my back up straight. "I hope you don't think I'm making this up."

He stepped into the craft. "I believe something happened here. I need to figure out what." Slowly, he turned a full circle, and then he wiped up the water, folded the towel, and laid it on the seat. "Nice boat."

"It's the fastest boat on the lake. I should have followed them."

Jake's eyebrows went up. "That would have been foolish."

"I could have caught up," I huffed back. "I might have found out who it was."

He scowled at me. "You want to join that guy at the bottom of the lake?" Then he shook his head and said gruffly, "You did the right thing."

Just as those words left Jake's mouth, the sound of an approaching boat boomed across the water.

Sam Fitzpatrick, the owner of Sam's Resort, stood on the fly bridge of his thirty-five-foot white cabin cruiser. He throttled back and brought it in beside our dock. Scuba tanks lay on the stern deck, and a couple of men in black dive suits sat in the cabin, out of sight until they were right beside us. I told Sam where the skier went down. The boat reversed, turned, and headed back out. Jake pulled out a handkerchief, ironed and folded into a crisp square, and waved it when Sam reached the right place. I watched the divers buckle on their tanks and walk off the swim step into the water. They were visible for less than fifteen seconds.

"What do you know about the depth out there?" Jake asked.

"Not much. The only shallow spot is right here, close to shore. When we were kids, we were allowed to swim out about thirty feet." I gestured toward the high bank above us. "After that, I think the bottom keeps going down as steep as the hillside."

Jake nodded. "I expect so." He gazed at the hill, drawing his shaggy brows down to shade his eyes, then peered at the water.

I pointed at a spot a little way beyond the swimming area. "When Bill Harlan was a teenager, he sank his runabout over there. My brother and a bunch of girls—too many for the size of the boat—were out with him and a storm came up. The waves were over three feet high and they swamped it." Tom hadn't wanted his kid sister to go along, so I stayed ashore and pouted. "They barely made it that far before it went down. They all swam to the dock and as soon as they were safe, Dad lined them up and blistered their ears." I still felt smug about that.

Jake grinned.

"Anyway, Bill's boat lodged on a rock seventy feet down, and after a while, a diver floated it up."

We began to climb the stairs, all one hundred and three of them. Bear and I set a brisk pace. I expected Jake to fall behind, but he reached the top two steps behind me, and no shorter of breath. I wiped sweat off my forehead. "Not many geezers can keep up with me."

Jake leaned his arms on the railing and gazed at the lake. "Here's what I think: Our killers know the lake. They know these cabins are usually vacant right now, but to be sure, they came by and checked your place out before you got here last night. I guarantee they went to Cowans' and Peppers' as well. Right now, they think they've committed the perfect crime."

"I can't believe anyone who belongs here would do it. They could have chosen this spot by dumb luck."

"Maybe."

I noticed that Sam had made a show of starting to fish near the entrance to the bay, slowly trolling back and forth. The placid surface hid all trace of the divers and the body below. Everything looked totally normal. "Do you expect them to find the body?"

"I'll be surprised." His phone rang. "Jake." Color rose in his permanently tanned cheeks and he pressed his lips together. "Hell and damnation, Orlando." He

26

began to pace the deck, listening and grunting "Yeah" from time to time into the phone. "Okay. Look, you stay put. I'll go." He scowled as he hung up and turned to me. "Something's come up. Another problem. In the meantime, there's a deputy out on the road. He'll keep an eye on you."

Poking his pencil into the coil and stuffing his note pad into his pocket, he started toward the path around the cabin; then turned and pointed a long, heavily knuckled finger at me. "I'll be back. Stay put. Anything happens, call 911."

Chapter Four

Jake retreated along the side of the cabin, his feet crunching the gravel path in a vigorous pace. I watched him go, wondering whether I dared lock up and leave. Finally, ignoring the temptation to run away, I marched into the kitchen, grabbed my script, and went back to the deck. I would focus. I mentally marked out a stage and got to work, determined not to let what happened deter me from my goal to totally eclipse that witch Victoria at the audition.

Not only would I take the role of Kate in *The Taming of the Shrew,* I would be the flirtiest, feistiest, funniest Kate ever.

I stumbled over my opening lines three times in a row, and after that, it didn't get a lot better. I was neither fun nor exciting, and I definitely was *not* sexy. My Kate had less sparkle than stale champagne. At the back of my mind, theater reviews flashed on and off, "Heather Shelton bombs," and "If you insist on attending *Taming of the Shrew*, take your knitting."

I flung myself into the chair I'd used at breakfast, gazed up at a huge, fuzzy cocoon on the underside of the umbrella, and thought scorching, scathing thoughts about Alex St. John—that elegant, charming, heart-breaking son of a bitch.

Why had I let him talk me into auditioning?

Why? Because up until a couple of weeks ago, he

made me feel talented—brilliant even, and confident that I could do anything I put my mind to. I thought I could produce a stunning performance. That's why.

I fell in love with that man, something no woman should do. I thought he loved me back. And, if he loved me, then I must be something special. I was stupid. I mistook the excitement in his gray-blue eyes for love. It turned out to be nothing more than fascination with a new conquest.

A sharp crack came from the side of the cabin. I scrambled to my feet, my heart beating double time, my head light and dizzy. Bear padded out from under the table and looked at me. I gripped his collar. For several moments, we listened. Nothing. There was only one thing to do. I snatched a knife off the table and tiptoed along the deck, hugging the wall of the cabin. I pressed myself flat against the rough cedar wall. Then, before I could chicken out, I took a deep breath and stuck my head around the corner.

A few feet away, a squirrel paused halfway up the trunk of a small pine. I squinted into the shadows under the low-hanging branches. I scanned the trees that bordered the walkway and the driveway all the way up to the road. Nothing. My heart still thudded against my ribs. I frowned at Bear, who seemed to think we should pack up and go home.

"We've never been scared to stay here alone, Bear, and we aren't going to start now. If you fall off a bicycle, you don't get scared and you don't give up. You get right back on and pedal that sucker. That's what we're going to do, Bear. Pedal."

I headed for the stairs down to the dock. If someone *was* lurking out there in the trees, before they could get to me, I'd jump into Dad's boat. "Sticks, Bear." My faithful dog raced me down the steps.

I kept my eyes wide open as I selected a stick from a pile behind the boathouse and threw it as hard as I could. It arced out over the sapphire water, twisting end over end. Immediately, Bear launched himself, stretching his sturdy body out in a long curve, landing with a massive splash and sending up a shower of icy diamonds. He swam out vigorously, shoulder muscles alternately bunching up under his black fur, and when he turned back, he proudly carried the branch between his jaws.

Sam's boat came in to the middle of the bay and stopped. He shut off the engines and for a few minutes, everything was still. Then two black heads broke the surface. Kneeling on the swim step, Sam pulled up the divers' tanks, thumping them onto the deck. The divers handed up their fins, climbed aboard, and in another minute, men and gear were out of sight. Sam started the engines and turned toward the mouth of the cove.

"Hey," I yelled. "What about me?" But Sam was already on his way.

I wondered what Jake might do if I left. Could he arrest me? Throw me in jail? I couldn't decide either to leave or to stay. In a surreal daze, I threw the whitened old branch. I watched it spin against the cloudless sky over and over, until my shoulder hurt. Each time Bear clamped it firmly in his jaws and dropped it at my feet. If the murderers returned, those same jaws would break their arms.

Finally, I rested, sitting on the edge of the dock, smelling wet dog and listening to the gentle shush of ripples against the rocks. I gazed down through the crystal water at the pebbles and rocks on the bottom. I wondered who the water-skier was, who could possibly have thought it was a good idea to kill him, and why.

A boat appeared from up-lake, heading in my direction. My breath caught. I jumped up and started for the stairs. But then I recognized Bill Harlan. He had fished in our cove every summer that I could remember. When we were kids, he and my brother spent hours in his runabout, and sometimes they brought sweet, clean-tasting lake trout up to the cabin for lunch. Bill's first boat, the one he swamped near our dock, was bare aluminum with an outboard motor. Over the years, it was followed by a series of others, each one better, faster, sleeker.

Bill himself had gone the other way. He'd been pretty buff as a teenager, but recently he'd put on weight, grown a doughnut around the middle. No matter. At that moment, he looked like my dearest friend. I hopped up and down on the dock and waved both arms.

He stowed his fishing rod and zoomed toward me, ruffling his light brown hair. He wore shorts and a polo shirt, as usual. "Heather, that you?" Close in, he cut the engine and coasted right up to the dock. "Hey, Bear." His boat looked identical to Dad's, and it was brand new, so I knew it wasn't cheap. He grabbed a cleat and held on. "Hey, what's up? Been here long?"

I sat down and put my bare feet inside the boat to help hold it in place. "Am I glad to see a friendly face. You'll never believe . . .." Jake's admonition popped into my head and I clapped my hand over my mouth. "You have to swear you won't tell a soul."

He raised his right hand. "I so swear."

"If Sheriff O'Toole ever finds out, he'll skin me."

His eyebrows shot up over the rims of his dark glasses. "No worries."

"Early this morning, a couple of guys ran down a water-skier with their boat—right out there." I pointed.

Bill's spine jerked up straight. The color drained from his face. "Whoa!" He shook his head. "Don't tell me this." He looked the way I felt, shocked and pale.

"They smashed right into him, Bill. I saw it."

"Come on. Who would do that?"

"Nobody we know. Right?"

"Absolutely not." He pulled off his sunglasses. His pale blue eyes stared into mine. "You couldn't see who it was, huh?"

"There was little light, and it came from behind them, so they were in silhouette." I stretched my thumb and forefinger apart. "About this big."

"Were they talking? Did you hear anything?"

"Not really. The waves made too much noise."

"How about the boat?"

"I couldn't see that very well either."

He slipped his sunglasses back on. His round cheeks puffed as he let out a big sigh. "Good thing, actually, for your sake."

I shivered. "D'you think they'll come back?"

"Nah." He shook his head. "If they had any idea you were here, they wouldn't have left."

"In other words, they would have taken care of me on the spot."

"Exactly. You can bet on it." He rubbed a hand across the plump folds under his chin. "Man, it makes me think of some of the dumb stuff we used to do, me and Tom. But we never ran into anyone." He reached for the starter, then sat back. "Look, I've got to go to the office soon, so what else? Could you see any markings on the boat, anything to identify these guys?"

I shook my head. "Nothing. The boat looked like a gazillion others. I have no clue what kind it was."

"Did anyone else see it? Who's here with you?"

"I came alone."

"No boyfriend, huh?" His tone sounded a trifle too hearty, as if I were still Tom's pesky kid sister.

I ignored the dig about the boyfriend.

He went on, "Okay, I'd say you have nothing to worry about. But if you feel a little lonesome or get scared or anything, just whistle. Or come on over. I mean it."

My gut relaxed a tiny bit. "Thanks."

He shoved away from the dock and started the motor. "Someone took my old boat while I was at work a couple of days ago. I was going to fix it up a bit and sell it."

"What if they stole it and then used it to kill the guy? Then it would be traced to you."

"I've been thinking it's kids and they'd probably bring it back in a day or two, but you never know. I'd better call Jake." He patted the wheel. "I've had this baby three weeks now. After I saw your dad's, I had to have one like it. Boys and their toys, huh?" The engine's smooth, throaty idle grew as he opened the throttle. He turned and sped away.

I sat on the dock with my arm around Bear's neck.

Fine. Leave me here to face the killers alone.

Chapter Five

Over Lake Sterling, the afternoon silence stretched to infinity. Everyone with even a tiny grain of sense had long since settled into comfy lounge chairs with a good book. The clunk of cowboy boots on the wood deck jolted me out of a deep sleep. I jerked upright. I had crashed at the table with my head on my script. Now my neck hurt, and page ten of Act One was slimy and wet with drool.

Jake pretended not to notice as he sat down opposite me, but a little grin on his craggy features gave him away. I decided to ignore it. My brain felt far too foggy to come up with something clever to say.

The dark cast to his jaw reminded me that he'd been at work since early morning. Nonetheless, his shirt retained its creases and his posture was as erect as ever. "How about looking at some pictures?"

I rubbed my face with both hands. "Pictures?"

Jake opened a manila envelope. "Mug shots, so to speak." He pulled out a handful of eight by ten black and white photographs of boats. "I'll show them to you one at a time, quickly. Just look and tell me if any of them jump out at you." He laid the first in front of me.

I barely had time to blink before he put another on top, then another. I scanned each one. Nothing jumped, hopped, or even twitched—until number ten landed in front of my face. My heart rate soared. Suddenly wide awake, I put my finger on the photo.

Without a pause, he added several more. Then another that looked similar to the tenth. I tapped it. And the next. When the last one covered all the rest, he picked up the stack and pulled out the first one I'd chosen. "This looked familiar to you?"

I squinted at it. "It seemed almost exactly right, until I saw those other two." I pulled it closer. "Could I see them side by side?"

He placed them in front of me and leaned back casual like, but I felt his attention was focused on my face, watching.

Two were indeed the same model, one older than the other. The third was a different make, but had a similar profile. They all looked like good family boats, perfect for water skiing and fishing. "Jake, there's nothing distinctive about them. We've owned two boats that look like that, and so have a gazillion other families. The lake is thirty miles long. There must be dozens of them."

"Exactly."

"So how will you find it?"

Jake scratched his head, making the graying hair above his ear stick up. "Now, if I had run someone down, I'd clean my boat inside and out. I'd make sure there were no cracks in the bow, nothing to hold a tuft of hair or a bit of skin. Then I'd sit tight—have a beer, go to work, whatever I'd normally do; and I'd have a real good chance to get away with it. So, I'm hoping these guys will get a good case of the jitters. Maybe they'll try to get rid of the boat—maybe trailer it out or scuttle it, or haul it and paint it some other color." His mouth tightened into a grim line. "The more they try to outsmart me, the more clues they'll leave. Some idiots might as well leave highway signs."

"Some don't." I leaned my elbows on the table. "There's that little problem you found in the orchard this spring. The body you can't or won't talk about."

His eyes glinted. "This time, I have a material witness, and a much earlier start. No clue, no matter how small, will be overlooked. At any time, I may need to talk to you, so don't even think about leaving." He tapped my arm with the manila envelope. "Savvy?"

I gulped. "Did Bill Harlan call you today?"

His voice turned harsh. "Why?"

"His old boat was stolen from his dock a couple of nights ago."

"Where did you hear this? When?"

I had to confess. If there was one thing I'd learned, it was that bad news does not improve with time. "Bill was out fishing. And he came in to chat."

Jake scowled.

"And I—I told him. This morning, after Sam left."

I didn't have to look at Jake's face twice and rushed on, as if I didn't know I'd made a big faux pas. "It'd make sense to steal Bill's boat and use it to kill the guy. Then sink it, or maybe blow it up." I made large fountain-like movements with my arms. "Or take it back to his dock. Then *he'd* look guilty."

All the friendliness left Jake's eyes. They looked hard and cold. "Indeed."

My insides quaked. I felt pretty sure he was thinking we were no longer on the same team. I could see myself in handcuffs. I snapped my fingers, and Bear came to stand beside me. "He promised to keep quiet."

Jake got up and stomped back and forth for a

while, then he leaned his back against the railing, crossed his arms on his chest, and glared at me. "Whom else have you told?"

I knew I deserved the look, but, geez. I'm not a total airhead. "No one."

He pressed his lips together until they made a narrow line. After a very long minute, he turned around to look at the lake.

I was certain he was going to put me in jail. My heart started to thump against my ribs. "Maybe it's a good thing that I told Bill. I think his old boat looked like those photos."

He ignored me.

My mouth wouldn't stop jabbering. "Maybe he can find out who stole it. Then, there you are—a clue."

Still facing the water, Jake pulled out his phone and dialed.

It surprised me to see Sam's cabin cruiser down there. To the west, trees that stood like sentinels atop the bluff cast long, dark blue shadows across the cove. It must be after four o'clock already. How long had Sam been there? What else might have happened while I slept?

Jake headed for the stairs to the lake. "Come on down to the dock." Bear went with him, not half a step behind. "The divers want to ask what you know about the currents in here."

I called Bear to my side, grabbed his collar, and followed.

Sam motored toward us. Grinning, he held up a couple of lake trout. As he coasted in to the dock, he climbed down from the fly bridge and tossed Jake a mid-ship line. Jake caught the line and stooped to cleat it. Sam Fitzpatrick was about Jake's age, of medium height and build. Under a broad-brimmed hat, his bright blue eyes sparkled out of a lined, deeply tanned face.

One of the divers came out of the cabin onto the stern deck. "Howdy," he said.

He leaned over and shook Jake's hand, but he was looking at me. He wore shorts and a sweatshirt with no sleeves. A ponytail pulled wet hair off his face and revealed the beginnings of a receding hairline. He was half a head taller than Sam, had well-defined muscles under golden brown skin, and his eyes were a to-die-for hazel. His wide smile displayed deep dimples in both cheeks. Good thing I'm immune to charming men.

"Hi, Heather."

A little too late, Jake's introduction registered in my brain. I glanced at him for help, which he gave me with a hint of a grin. "You're Heather. He's Dave."

"Right." I faked a smile and stuffed my hands into the front pockets of my shorts. Who *was* this guy?

Dave leaned his back against the cabin and crossed one bare ankle over the other. "I hear you know this place better than anyone, Heather. Is there much of a current? Is there a chance a body could drift toward shore?"

"The lake flows from west to east, and an eddy swirls around in here." I drew a clockwise circle in the air. "The current isn't strong, but it could push it in." I shrugged. "It could also pull it back out."

"That's what I thought." Dave shifted his gaze to Jake. "This morning, the guys laid out a grid with yellow line and numbered each sector. This afternoon, we searched sector by sector and covered about half of the grid. Unfortunately, after a hundred and twenty feet, the bottom drops off sharply. It goes way below our range and most likely that's where it would be, unless the current carried it in. If there is a body."

My hands fisted on my hips. What did he mean, *if* there is a body?

Jake frowned. "Gotcha." He prodded a cleat with the toe of his boot. "What's it like down there?"

"It's mostly a steep, rocky slope scored with crevices. There are occasional flat spots, and those are littered with rocks and boulders."

"How's the light?"

"In the middle of the day, when the sun is overhead, it's pretty good until you get past ninety feet, but now it's really dark down there, especially on the west side." He hooked his thumb back over his shoulder. "And our lights have a limited range, so it's slow going."

Jake nodded. "Sounds as if you need to take another look. How about tomorrow?"

Dave glanced at Sam, who had gone back up to the fly bridge and started the engines, but leaned over the handrail, listening. Sam said, "Tomorrow's Saturday so it will be busy at the resort, but Penny can handle it."

Dave gave a thumbs up. "I'll try to get bigger lights. Those crevices are blacker than Lady MacBeth's heart."

I started at his reference to the Bard. It didn't fit the stereotype of a man who makes a living diving. He was looking at me, and I realized he'd caught me staring at him. He grinned and turned back to Jake. "I'll get in the water any time, especially on someone else's dime."

"It's a deal." Jake slipped the line off the cleat and tossed it as Sam started away from the dock.

Dave snaked out a hand to catch it. "Take care."

Jake turned to me. "Must I remind you that you're not to speak of this to anyone?"

I bunched my hands into fists. "I got it the first time. It's just that Bill feels like family. Besides, he isn't stupid. And he knows everybody. He might hear something that will help you."

"Okay. Truce. No use crying over spilled milk. But you'd better hope he's kept it to himself."

We watched until Sam was far enough away from the dock to head for open water and put on some speed. The shadows darkened the cove. The afternoon was coming to an end without even one solid clue. My head ached. I could feel my shoulders slump. This was all wrong. "It's going to end up another mystery, like the body in the orchard."

Jake marched back up the dock. "If I believed that, I'd be hanging out at Rosie's eating donuts." He paused at the foot of the stairs, motioned for me to go ahead.

The steps looked much too steep to climb, but I forced myself to set a brisk pace in order not to appear the wimp. Not when there was a geezer behind me. Jake lagged behind. Bear the Fickle chose to stay with him.

Back on the deck, I folded the umbrella down and fastened the Velcro strip around it. I went inside, closed the wooden shutters that cover the sliding glass door, and spun the wing nut onto the bolt that fastened them together. Then I slid the glass door shut. I went through the kitchen, stepped out the back door, and locked it. Jake and Bear met me there.

Jake glanced at the duffel bag in my hand and raised his eyebrows. "You going to town?"

"I think I'll stay at Robin Westover's."

"Excellent. You know her from Seattle?"

"Right. She lived next door to me when we were kids." I walked into the carport and put my bag on Bogey's back seat.

"Good idea. If that doesn't pan out, Sam's Resort isn't full. He could put you up. And by the way, it's okay to talk to him. Only him, mind you. He's been my buddy since 'Nam." Jake's eyes narrowed and after a moment he continued, "We'd be hunkered down in a stinking, steaming trench with sweat rolling down our backs, and he'd be raving about the lake and the mountains and the cool, fresh air."

I nodded, barely listening. I felt as if I'd been at the helm of a star ship, crashing through space at warp speed all day, avoiding planets and meteors that came whizzing at me. I'd had no time to process it all. If I could be still for a while, maybe I could dredge up whatever it was that had been niggling at the back of my brain all day.

Although I ached for her sanity, I couldn't picture sitting on Robin's verandah, watching the antics of her toddler dressed in frilly pink and jabbering the way we usually did.

Chapter Six

I backed Bogey out of the carport and followed Jake up the steep driveway to the road that undulated past our cabin, a narrow ribbon of asphalt drizzled onto the uneven rocky hillside. Jake turned right, in the direction of Bill Harlan's house and quickly disappeared over the next knoll. Acutely aware of being alone, I popped the clutch, catapulted Bogey up onto the pavement, and turned left, toward the town of Sterling.

Around the first corner, before I got to Cowans' driveway, I passed an old green pickup truck pulled off on the side. A man in khaki shorts and a red plaid shirt bent under the raised hood. I slowed down and yelled, "Need help?"

He shook his head, waved a wrench, and grinned.

I glanced in the rear-view mirror. My brain raced. Could that be the deputy? The guy who's been protecting me? Armed with a wrench? Seriously? It had to be. One more weird thing to cope with in a totally weird, totally scary day.

In order to get through it without falling apart, I'd compressed all my emotions into a frightened little knot in my chest that made it hard to take a deep breath. Now, every cell in my body wanted to drive straight to the highway, and not stop until I got to Seattle. I wanted to drink red wine and eat a whole pot of my friend

Janice's spaghetti and tell her everything. Janice was a great listener, the type of friend everyone should have. She never interrupted. She never told me what to do. And she wouldn't blab.

When I passed High Haven Marina, I glimpsed the red roof of the store through the trees. It seemed eons since I'd met Jake there. I reached over and grabbed a handful of Bear's hair. He sat on his haunches, let the wind blow on his face, and looked supremely pleased with himself.

I gazed at each cabin as I drove past. I read every name on every driveway. As eager as a thirsty camel coming upon an oasis in the desert, I drank in the familiar atmosphere. I crossed the Quarter Note River right where it began, as it flowed out of the lake, and then turned onto Sterling's main street. Everything looked exactly the way it always did. The street smelled hot and dusty. At the first intersection, I waited while a couple crossed in front of me. They were chatting, pushing a stroller, eating ice cream cones. The ordinariness of it all loosened the knot in my chest, and as it unraveled, suddenly, I felt ravenous. I angled into a parking place in front of the hardware store.

Bear looked dejected at being left in the car, but I had parked in the shade and the top was down, and people he knew would stop and say hi. Two doors down, at the Key of C, my favorite restaurant, I ran up the stairs to the rooftop deck. Plopping into a chair under an umbrella advertising my favorite beer, I looked over the railing at the river as it tumbled innocently on its way to meet and be swallowed up by the Columbia, then rush on to the Pacific. A few people meandered along the path in the narrow, green, riverside park. Two older couples sat on benches flanked by huge cement pots filled with bright orange and yellow flowers.

But my gaze returned to the peaceful, smoothly flowing water. I wondered if the current in our cove had carried the body out into the lake, if it would have drifted all the way down and into the river, and if, at any moment, it could possibly float right past all those people. I wondered if they would notice it going by.

I puzzled over who could have killed the skier, and whether this morning's murder could be related to the body in the orchard. That would make two killings— two killings that were somehow connected. In this quiet vacation community.

Part of me couldn't believe it. In all the years my family had been coming here, I had never heard of anyone being murdered. Perhaps the ladies' prayer group was right. They blamed a recent increase in crime on the casino a few miles out of town. It did bring a different set of people to Sterling, people who didn't actually belong. Everyone said that most likely, they preyed on each other. That made sense. They were not our friends and neighbors, so, we, ourselves, had nothing to fear. Still.

The clatter of high heels on the wide planks of the deck saved me the pain of further introspection. "Sorry," the server called, "I didn't realize you'd come up here." She wore a perky white camp shirt, a short denim skirt, and stiletto heels. Red stiletto heels. On a deck with gaps between the planks. Go figure.

She sped toward me as if born with those shoes on her feet, never once slipping into a crack or knothole. One hand held a menu and a napkin rolled up around a knife and fork, and in the other hand, she carried a stubby glass brimming with ice water. "Gosh, I hope you haven't been waiting long. I could have died when I came up to start the coffee and saw you sitting here."

Everything about her was little and cute and nicely proportioned, like Victoria, the red-clawed boyfriend snatcher. Even as a toddler, I was never petite and cute.

Her badge said her name was Mariella. "Y'know," she said, "some days start off wrong, and never do get going right."

Victoria always wore red, high-heeled shoes. I snatched the menu. "I didn't come here to listen to your problems."

"Sorry." Raising one eyebrow, Mariella turned and marched away.

Her cute little skirt wrapped snugly across her butt and wagged from side to side with each step. I reviewed my list of crimes du jour: watched murder and did nothing; disobeyed the sheriff and blabbed to Bill Harlan; felt sorry for self and made rude remark to an innocent server.

I sighed. If only I had taken Alex up on his offer to help me rehearse, I'd still be in Seattle. None of this would have happened. The problem was that one lock of black hair that always fell across his forehead. I'd push it away, and then his winter-sky eyes would soften, and he'd lean toward me, and his lips would . . ..

Geez, Heather, enough already.

In a minute Mariella was back. "Something to drink?" There was an expression in her eyes that made her seem older than I had first thought. It hinted that she'd seen a little too much of life.

I pointed at the umbrella. "I'd like one of those."

"Beer? No problem."

I knew what I wanted, but I read the menu anyway. It was safe and inoffensive, with pictures of ruffled lettuce escaping whole-grain bread.

Mariella brought my drink. "This will cheer you up. You were looking pretty gloomy when I came up here." She clapped a hand over her mouth. "Oops, there I go again."

I dredged up a smile and ordered my favorite sandwich, and she tottered away on those ridiculous and dangerous high heeled shoes.

The sun slid the first golden rays of evening under the umbrella and kissed my face with warmth. I took a long swallow of chilled lager, licked my lips to taste the lingering tartness of the wedge of lime, and leaned back in my chair. Actually, Victoria had three different pairs of red boots that came up over her knees, all of them with very high heels. Eye catching. And man catching. It wasn't fair. For four glorious months, Alex and I had shared sunsets and ice cream cones and long, delicious nights together. That was a lot to give up without whimpering.

I had to stop thinking about Alex. And the body in the lake. Jake would reach out his long arms and drag the killers to justice. It was not my problem. My problem was to get ready for my audition. And the truth was, I would not be able to do that if I stayed at Robin's house.

Mariella plunked down a giant pastrami and Swiss sandwich with lettuce and tomatoes and accompanied by a huge mound of French fries that smelled crisp and hot—divine. I picked up my sandwich with both hands and leaned my elbows on the table. I didn't care that the tomatoes kept falling out.

I'd worked hard on my acting skills all winter, hoping to play Kate. Every minute that I wasn't peering into teenage mouths while working in my father's dental office as his hygienist, I volunteered at the theater and practiced and dreamed of landing this prime role. I wasn't going to give up now.

I still had two days to get ready for auditions. I could do it if I went back to the cabin and knuckled down. I'd been scared to death there, but that didn't mean it wasn't safe. As Bill said, if the bad guys had known I was there, I'd be dead already. Therefore, they didn't know. Plus, if I parked my car next door in the Cowans' carport, I could walk to our place by the connecting footpath. Then, if I kept the shutters closed on the cabin, no one would ever know I was inside. And if anything happened, I had Bear, one hundred and five pounds of well-trained teeth, claws, and muscles. Besides, Bill Harlan was only a few minutes away.

Mariella headed for my table, balancing her tray. "Everything okay?"

I shook my head. "I want to apologize for snapping at you earlier."

Her smile returned instantly. "It's okay. I could tell you were unhappy. Guy problems, I just bet. Everybody has them. I mean, gosh, look at me." She went to the serving bar, picked up a tray of salt and pepper shakers, set them on the table next to mine, and started wiping them with a damp white cloth. "My boyfriend stood me up today. We were only going to meet for coffee, but still." She rolled her eyes. "Here I am, killing myself in these stupid shoes in case he drops by to apologize." She slipped one shoe off and wiggled her toes.

I tackled the fries. "You want to look good."

"My roommate says I should tell him to bugger off." She paused, a salt shaker in her hand, and looked into the distance. "But he's different. He's smart and funny and he's got class, like his car, for instance. He's older, see, but not too old, and like, well, y'know how it is when a guy treats you real special?"

I did know—and tried not to stare at the hickey on her neck. "Have you known him long?"

"Four days. See, he stopped to help me change my tire in the pouring rain the other day. Then he took me to dinner." Hustling from table to table, she put out the shakers. "If you see a hunk in a racy red sports car, that's Ken—Ken Lagazo. And remember, I have dibs on him."

I paid at the cash register downstairs. I gripped my purse, my keys, and my determination. Looking over my shoulder every two seconds, I started back to the cabin. I almost forgot our traditional ice cream, but as we approached G & G's country store, Bear reminded me. I turned into the dusty parking lot and stopped in the shade of the weathered wood building. Bear shifted his weight from paw to paw, kneading the seat. I got out of the car. "Stay."

A slight blonde woman bounced down the steps from the store. She tossed me a carefree smile, said "Hi," and hustled into a battered pickup truck with orchard ladders in the back.

I usually felt carefree, too, when I was at the lake. Everyone did. Except maybe the mothers of small children. I wandered into the store and stared at the freezer case. Could I be wrong about what I witnessed that morning? Was it really premeditated murder?

"I recommend the mocha fudge."

I jumped. Behind the counter, George, a wiry guy a couple of inches shorter than me, wiped his hands on his white apron and grinned. I was dying to ask him if he thought anyone who belonged at the lake, as we did, would commit murder.

Instead, I said, "Anything happening today?"

He smoothed his handlebar mustache. "Nope. Same ol' same ol'."

While he scooped mocha fudge into a little round container, I chose a quart of milk from the refrigerator. Suppose George caught Gabby, his wife, sneaking around with some other man. Would he kill the guy? George whistled "Unchained Melody" as he wrapped my ice cream in newspaper to keep it cold. No, no, and no. Not George. Not anyone.

"Bet you need a couple of woofers." He reached behind the counter and brought out two cat-shaped, homemade dog biscuits and handed them to me along with my change.

The woofers felt like coarse, greasy sandpaper. As I came out of the store, Bear sprang from the front seat to the back and stood with his paws on the folded-down convertible top, quivering.

With a silent apology to cats everywhere, I balanced a woofer on Bear's nose. He drooled and shivered, but the cookie stayed put. "Okay." Tossing his head, he flipped it into the air and caught it in his mouth. It lasted about three seconds. I scratched his ears. He looked at me with such longing, I had to give him the other one.

Time to get serious. If I was going to be the best Kate ever, I needed to work on my timing. In the theater arts class I'd taken from Alex, I'd learned the importance of giving the audience time to react. If I wanted the audience to laugh, to cheer, and to love me, then I had to break my habit of rushing my lines.

At auditions next Tuesday, I needed to dazzle the director, Donovan. My friend Janice was right. She kept telling me, "You have to remember that Griffin Donovan has no balls. He knows Victoria's work and it's good. Vanilla, but good. He will be inclined to settle for that, so if you want him to pick you instead, you have to knock his silk socks off."

I was so busy thinking about what Janice said, I nearly forgot my plan to leave Bogey in the Cowans' carport. I remembered just in time to turn in. Outspoken environmentalists, the Cowans had saved as many trees as they could, and because the driveway twisted through tightly packed pine forest, it was long and bumpy. I geared Bogey down and jostled along until I pulled in beside their cabin.

Bear trotted around the edges of the concrete floor, sniffing. A winter's worth of pine needles and cones had gathered in the corners. It looked as if no one had been there in months. With my duffel in one hand, and the sack from G and G's in the other, I started along the trail. Under towering pines, needles carpeted the forest floor. It was cool and dusky. Some of the wild asparagus, which we had roasted on Memorial Day, had started to put out fern-like growth. I wished I could turn back the calendar and restart the day. Or the week. Even the whole month.

As I neared our place, my pace slowed. I stopped, feeling the heavy beat of my heart under my collarbone. What if someone was there? Should I turn around?

Bear started to go ahead. "Sit," I said.

I peered through the last few trees at the cabin. I'd left the sliding doors and all the windows shuttered. Up on the deck, I saw the picnic table with the umbrella folded down. Nothing changed. We were alone.

I took a deep breath. "Heel." We hurried around to the back door, stepped into the kitchen, and slid the dead bolt into place. Leaning against the door, I sighed. It felt good to be alone and quiet. Bear trotted to his water dish and began slurping. Light entered via skylights on the roof and countered the darkness imposed by the shutters. From where I stood, I saw the living room on the other side of the eating bar—the sofa, the round enameled fireplace, and the soft white drapes.

I reminded myself that during the afternoon, I'd charged my phone, made sure I got a dial tone, and written Bill Harlan's phone number on the same pad of paper that Mom used for her grocery lists. I was silly to worry. I could do this. And it was only seven o'clock. I had lots of time.

I marched to the living room and shoved the sofa back against the eating bar, visualized the stage and began. Hours went by. My character became so real to me, I felt the period costumes with their elaborate layered petticoats bumping against my ankles as I strode around my stage. Once, I got so carried away that I ran into the fireplace and bruised my shin.

My timing was perfect. Kate sparkled. She shone. She won the hearts of the audience. Finally, I took my bows and came back to the real world.

From the freezer, I heard the call of mocha fudge ice cream. I opened the carton, found a spoon, and plunked down on the sofa. With my feet stretched out on the seat, I leaned back against the armrest and savored every bite. On Tuesday, I was going to blow dear director Griffin Donovan away. He would never know what hit him. I didn't need Alex's help. I could fly with my own wings. Visions of audiences leaping to their feet, shouting "Brava!" shimmered in my mind.

Grandma Garnet would be the first on her feet. Even my mother would follow suit.

While there was still a spoonful of ice cream left, I called Bear. Generally, I don't give him chocolate, but this was a special moment. He hunkered down on the floor with the container between his paws. I closed my eyes to rest them.

When Bear nudged me awake, his nose was three inches from mine. I closed my eyes. But he put one paw up on my stomach. Then I smelled it—a faint trace of cigarette smoke. I jerked up straight, heart pounding.

Bear stood by the sofa, alert and on guard. "What is it?" I whispered.

After a minute, I wondered if I had imagined the smell, but then I heard a slight scuff, the sound of a foot on the deck, a few feet from where I sat. Twisting my fingers into the hair on the back of Bear's neck, I sat absolutely still, afraid that if I moved, my shadow would fall across the cracks in the shutters. I couldn't get my breath. I stared at the sliding glass door, reassuring myself that I had locked it, that the shutters covering it were bolted from the inside, and that I'd locked and bolted the kitchen door. No one could see in. No one would know I was there.

There was a thud as the shutter pushed against the bolt. Bear tensed. I wrapped my arms around his neck and thanked my lucky stars that he wouldn't bark. I practically strangled the poor dog.

Eternities passed. I told myself that Dad had constructed the place so soundly that they'd have to chop their way in with an ax. I'd have time to escape and run like hell to my car. Immobile, we waited. My heart thumped so hard against my ribs, I thought for sure they'd hear it.

The kitchen doorknob clicked. The dead bolt clunked. They had gone around the cabin. I crept to the kitchen. I put my keys in my pocket. I grabbed my phone. If they got in, Bear would attack. He has enough speed and strength to knock a large man down. And his jaws are powerful enough to snap a man's arm in two. The only thing that could stop him would be a bullet.

I pushed 9, then 1-1.

A woman's voice, calm, quiet, said, "What is your emergency?"

I stage whispered, "Someone is outside, prowling around the cabin."

"You're on a cellphone. Where are you?"

I heard a sharp crack. Splinters of wood flew into the kitchen. I couldn't speak. All I could remember was my address on Corliss Avenue in Seattle.

"You must be in Sterling County. Where?"

The door thumped against the frame, as if someone had put their shoulder against it and pushed. I clung to the sound of the voice on the phone. "Tell Jake the killer is shooting at the door!"

I ran to the deck door, unlocked the sliding glass door and shoved it open. I fumbled with the wing nut holding the shutters. Two more sharp cracks followed. Another thud. The sound of splintering wood. I spun the nut off the shutter. More shots. I yanked the shutter aside. Behind me, the kitchen door crashed to the floor.

My feet barely touched the deck as I sped over it. In seconds, I was across the driveway, between the trees, on the trail to the Cowans' place. Feet pounded on the deck behind me. Bear ran ahead. The trail disappeared in blackness. I wanted to call Bear back, but I could see the white tip of his tail, swaying from side to side in front of me, and my feet knew the way. With my gaze fixed on that speck of white, I plunged forward.

Behind me, twigs cracked. Light flickered through the branches. Not far behind, a man chuckled. That chuckle—I'd heard it that morning from the boat—full of pleasure. My heart nearly stopped.

"Run, bitch," he called, amusement rippling through the words. "Run all you like."

I couldn't get enough air. I stumbled, lost my rhythm, lost a valuable second or two. But the trees began to thin out and a faint beam of moonlight shone in the clearing ahead. Bear's dark shape became visible. He'd reached the end of the trail and turned, waiting for me. The Cowans' cabin was a hundred yards away.

"In the car." I dragged the keys out of my pocket, sprinted into the carport, and yanked open the door. We jumped in. My hands shook. I tried to put the key in the ignition and missed.

A beam of light swung across the carport. He had reached the clearing. The key slid into place, and Bogey started on the first try. I backed out onto the driveway, cramping the wheel to turn around. I went forward and then had to reverse again. The flashlight beam caught my eyes, blinding me. He'd reached the carport. I had no choice. "Bear. Rip him up."

Bear leaped. I heard a shout. The white blaze on Bear's forehead glowed red, reflecting my taillights. The man was flat on the concrete. Bear's jaws hovered over his neck.

"Fuck you," I yelled. "Bear, come." I popped the clutch just as Bear jumped in. The tires spun, spraying gravel. I hoped it peppered the SOB. I hoped it blinded him. I hoped it knocked his teeth out. With a sweaty palm on the gear shift, I shoved it into second and we bounced up the driveway.

In the distance, I heard a siren. "We did it. We're okay now, Bear. We're almost to the road."

Bogey skidded around a massive pine and right into the grill of a big, black, shiny truck that blocked the drive. "Oh, shit. Oh, God." For a second, I stared at it, unbelieving. I backed up, searching for a way through the trees. On both sides, the majestic trunks blocked the way. From behind, I heard that horrible laugh. Light washed the branches around me.

Pushing my shoulder against the door, I swung it open and jumped out. "Come, Bear." We ran around the SUV. Which way should I go? Right—uphill toward the deputy? But was he still there? I turned left, downhill, toward town, toward the siren. My feet slipped and slid in my sandals. I kicked them off and ran hard, safe for a moment from eyes that would see my white shirt and the tip of Bear's tail.

Far ahead, the siren shrilled through the night. I tried to pick out a hiding place, but the bank was too steep. On my right, a sheer rock wall went up. On my left, the hill fell away in a steep ravine. Behind me, the SUV roared to life. My heart jumped to my throat. Out in the lake, still a good distance away, pulsing red lights reflected up at the starry sky. Behind us, the truck accelerated, coming after me.

We were close to the beginning of the wedge-shaped concrete guardrail. Suddenly it loomed, very near. If we could get down behind it . . .. My feet beat steadily on the white line.

The SUV sounded so close I glanced back. Searing, blinding pain ripped through my chest, and I couldn't get my breath. Vaguely, I felt myself punted high over the ravine. Somewhere inside, I knew my muscles had been torn from my bones. My arms and legs hung limp and useless from my arching body, and I tumbled into the soft black night.

Chapter Seven

The primitive urge that pushed the first man to his feet roused me, it's message loud and clear: *Danger lurks in the shadows. Wake up. Move. Be aware.*

I opened my eyes. Horizontal bands of sunshine slanted through partially open blinds, casting alternating bars of light and shade on the walls. Someone had taped my arm to a padded board. Bright green lines scrolled across a monitor at the side of my bed. I tried to make sense of everything but thinking hurt too much. Everything hurt too much so I gave up.

"Heather. Heather," a voice rumbled. The graveled tone sounded familiar. "It's Jake O'Toole." He sat beside my bed, leaning forward and peering at me, and he seemed to be . . . glowing.

"Are you an angel?" Later, the doctor assured me that the sheriff's silvery glow did not come from some sort of saintly status, but from the swelling in my brain.

"Jake O'Toole." He paused, then continued, "I'm the sheriff. Can you tell me what happened?"

"I don't know."

"I believe you were running or walking, and you were in an accident. Do you remember?"

I tried to form an answer, but I felt myself drifting. Like a kaleidoscope, nightmares and dreams merged into one, then splintered into jagged fragments. The next time I woke, I knew I was in the little hospital at

Sterling, but didn't know why. My head ached. My back ached. In fact, my whole body ached. I put a hand to my face, and it felt puffy, swollen, so swollen one eye wouldn't open.

A man, a stranger, sat beside the door. When I turned my head to get a better look at him, the room spun. He came to the side of my bed. "I've been waiting for you to come around." His voice sounded like liquid chocolate, the kind a woman could wake up to every day. It would be easy to look at him over morning coffee, too. He had even white teeth, mocha skin, curly black hair, and dark, totally unfathomable eyes—the kind that hold secrets forever.

"I'm Deputy Angel Orlando."

I dragged my gaze away from his eyes long enough to notice the shining badge above his starched khaki pocket, and his lean, muscular body. Anyone who looked that good had to be a dream. I closed my eyes, but when I opened them again, he was still there.

"Why are you here?" My voice cracked. "Why am I here?" My mouth felt stiff and unused.

"You had an accident." He held a cup of water, bent the straw toward my mouth, and waited while I drank. "Can you remember what happened?"

"Bear!" My heart raced. I reached out and gripped the deputy's hand. "Where's my dog?"

"He's with Sheriff O'Toole."

"Is he . . .?"

"Bear is fine. Don't worry. O'Toole is taking good care of him." Deputy Orlando's eyes watched my face. "You were at your cabin. Then what happened?"

I heard the sound of my feet running, beating the pavement. My heart pounded something fierce because

58

something really bad was about to happen. But it made no sense. "I don't know."

Soft-soled shoes and quiet voices brushed through my consciousness. Conversations about urinary output and blood pressure, fractured ribs and liver damage danced in and out with the swish of footsteps and whispered consultations. If I took a deep breath, a knife stabbed through my chest. Once the pain quieted, I tried to get up, but my body weighed too much even though the head of the bed was elevated.

The next time I woke up, I felt as if I'd slept long and hard. The nurse who helped me walk to the bathroom announced that I was alert and oriented, as if I'd won a prize at the county fair. An aide helped me wash, then Angel Orlando with the gorgeous eyes came back in. He questioned me again. Obviously, he thought I knew something important.

"Why don't *you* tell *me*?" I demanded at last.

Angel smiled. "Sounds like you're feeling better," he said. "A couple of visitors have been waiting to see you, but before I let them come in, the sheriff insists that you tell everyone you were hit by a car while you were jogging."

"That's what happened?"

"That's what you must tell everyone." He paused, watching my face. "Agreed?"

"No, I do not agree." Seriously, it was all too much. "Why?"

"Sheriff O'Toole's orders. And I need to know that you understand and will comply, no matter what you do or do not remember."

I realized right then that a handsome man can be as irritating as a plain one. Maybe more. "I absolutely do not understand. But I will do as you ask."

A smile broke out over Angel's face. And despite my irritation, it was like sunshine in Seattle on a winter day. He opened the door and beckoned to someone in the hallway. Then he placed a chair beside my bed and sat down. "I'll be right here."

I rolled my eyes.

A pair of boys dressed in shorts and T-shirts came in and stopped at the foot of my bed. They were about eleven years old. The shorter one, stocky, red-haired and freckle-faced was Jordan Prescott. His mother, Mary, was a teacher in Seattle and spent summers at Sam's Resort. I'd known him since he was a baby. Both of them looked at me solemnly.

"Heather?" Jordan tipped his head to one side and peered at me. His forehead wrinkled in concern. "Holy cow. I can hardly recognize you. Are you okay?"

"I'm fine." When I tried to smile, my face felt too stiff to move. "I imagine I look a little scary, though."

Jordan nodded. "Not as scary as when we found you. Now that was—"

Inside my head, I heard the sounds of running feet. Real, or imagined? "You found me?"

"Yup. Me and Travis. This is my cousin." He tilted his head toward the tall, dark-haired boy beside him. "He gets to stay with us this summer."

Travis tied a helium balloon that said "Get well" to the end of the bed. He said, "We always get up early to go fishing, see, and Sam—he's our uncle or cousin or something—was checking out the dock, and the sheriff came and said he needed help to look for you."

"Yeah, we said we'd go," Jordan continued. "But Sam said we had to ask Mom, and she kills us if we wake her up. The rule is we have to wait until she's had a giant cup of coffee."

"You are so lucky we disobeyed," Travis said.

"Yeah," Jordan said. "We're grounded, but we don't care. You could be dead if we didn't. You were way down in the ravine, all bloody and tangled up in the bushes."

"Yeah," Travis said, all serious. "Jordy nearly puked."

Jordan pulled a rubber band out of his pocket and snapped his cousin on the arm with it. "We didn't know if you were dead or alive. Your dog wouldn't let us come close. But the sheriff came because he saw our bikes, and he knew Bear's name and everything. Plus, he called the ambulance. Hey, Trav, d'you think Mom would let me get a dog like him?" Jordan's eyes were wide and round. "Bear's awesome."

"Get real, Jordy. She hates dogs."

"She doesn't really. Besides, with all the bad stuff that's going on, we should have a dog like him."

"Bad stuff?" I asked.

"Okay, first of all, Sam found a dead body in the orchard," Jordan said. "And second of all, some crazy is going around, bumping off all you women."

Angel shifted in his chair. His eyebrows went up and he shot me a glance.

"Like, somebody ran over you," Travis offered, "then Mariella disappeared."

Something made my breath catch. "Mariella?" The name sounded familiar but I could not place her.

At that moment, the door opened and Jordan's mom, Mary Prescott, came in. In shorts and a T-shirt, with her auburn hair pulled back off her freckled face, she looked like another kid. Her husband is a friend of my father. We attended their wedding when I was thirteen, and I thought it was the most romantic moment I had ever witnessed: a bride only twelve years older than me, with a train a mile long, walking up the aisle to meet her love. Later, I realized she married someone as old as Dad, and that spoiled everything. But over the years, we've become friends.

I wanted to hear more about the missing woman Mariella, but Mary sent the boys outside to wait. "They've been worried about you," she said. "I have, too. And listen, I know your folks are in Europe, so when you get out of here, I want you to stay with me in my cabin at Sam's. You shouldn't be alone."

A lump blocked my throat and tears threatened. All I could say was, "Thank you."

"It's a deal." She squeezed my hand and then started for the door. "I have to go. I'm running late. Jake O'Toole is waiting to hear what the boys know about Mariella."

Mariella again.

Disappeared.

Who was she?

****

The third morning, when I woke up, I could actually open my mouth and chew a piece of toast. Not only that, but when I sipped my coffee—not as good as a cold-pressed dark roast, but it still tasted heavenly—it didn't run down my chin. It wasn't all sunshine, however. The chipper morning nurse told me it was Monday. And smiled, as if I should be happy about it.

Monday was the day before auditions. Suddenly, the coffee tasted old and burned. Clearly, I wasn't going to get there. But why? I still couldn't remember anything that had happened between driving over to the cabin and waking up in the hospital.

Just then, Jake O'Toole arrived. "Now, don't get in a tizzy," he said to the nurse. "This critter won't hurt your hospital. He wants to say hello to this young lady."

Bear bounded into the room and put his nose on the bed, right up beside me. As he wagged his whole rear end, I scratched his ears, and he smiled his goofy smile. If only he could stay there.

Before Jake started in I said, "Look, I need to know what's going on."

He nodded. "Now that you're a little better, I'll tell you. Friday morning, early, you witnessed a crime. You phoned me. I came out to the cabin and we talked."

"Truly?"

He looked at me. Said nothing, and waited.

"This Angel Orlando person has asked me what happened on Friday at least a dozen times, but I can't tell him anything."

"That evening," Jake said, "you told me you would stay in town with Robin Westover."

"I know Robin, and I often stop by to see her, but why would I stay with her? You must have been talking to someone else."

"It was you, Heather. You told me yourself." His lips formed a hard, firm line. "Then, at one-thirty in the morning, you phoned 911 from the cabin. By the time we got there, the door had been broken down, and you were gone. We found your car in the Cowans' driveway, motor running, headlights on, bumper smashed in."

My heart stopped. My brother had handed Bogey

down to me when I was a junior in college, like a rite of passage, against my mother's wishes.

"Smashed?" I loved my little old car, almost as much as I loved Bear. What if it couldn't be fixed? "Is it bad? Why would Bogey be over at the Cowans'?"

"That's my line." His craggy face broke into a grin as he got to his feet. "I was hoping you could tell me. If you recall anything at all, tell Deputy Orlando immediately." He started across the room. "We fixed the cabin door, by the way. Say goodbye, Bear." My dog followed him out.

I tried hard to remember, but nothing came. I had no clue what had happened or why my car had been at Cowans'. What I knew for sure was that my mother would insist I buy a nice, safe, boxy, crossover vehicle like hers, and that tomorrow was Tuesday, when auditions would go on without me.

And that Bear had left me here alone.

For the rest of the morning, I cried my way through an entire box of tissues. I saw all my hard work circling the drain. I pictured Victoria in her thigh-high red boots, tumbled black curls in practiced disarray, phoney smile on her face, bright red claws wrapped around Alex's arm.

And grinning because the director gave her the role—my role.

It was so totally unfair.

****

At lunchtime that day, Bill Harlan came. With a navy jacket over his polo shirt and slacks, he looked as if he might be on his way to an important meeting. Angel Orlando stopped him at the door; made him remove his jacket and empty all his pockets.

Bill scowled. "Is this fucking necessary?"

The deputy asked him to spread his arms before he patted him down. "Thank you," he said, and picked up something that looked like a syringe. "What's this?"

"My insulin pen." Bill wiped sweat off his forehead. "Since when do you do pat a guy down on account of a hit and run?"

Angel uncapped the pen, turned it around in his hands, squirted a tiny stream into his palm. "That would be a question for Sheriff O'Toole."

He gave the pen back, and Bill put it in his pocket, looking like he was trying hard not to smack Angel. He waved some index cards at me. "I've got some really dangerous stuff here. My notes for a speech at Rotary— trying to convince them to finance a sailing club for low-income kids." He slid the cards into his pocket.

"Sorry," Angel said. "Sheriff's orders. All visitors and visits are to be monitored." He pulled his chair close to the bed and sat down as if he had nothing better to do on a sunny afternoon.

Bill moved to the window, looked out for a minute, then turned around and leaned against the sill. He crossed his arms on his chest and put one ankle over the other. "Look, Heather, I'm sorry, but Orlando here pissed me off. I heard you have amnesia. How come? What happened?"

"I don't know."

"I dropped by and chatted with you Friday morning. Remember?"

"You came to the cabin?"

"Yes." He ambled over and stood at the foot of the bed. "I was out fishing, you know, like Tom and I used to do, and you were down on the dock with Bear so I chugged in to say hi."

I scoured my brain, then shook my head. "To me, it never happened."

"Well, I remember clearly." Bill's voice resumed the teasing tone reserved for Tom's kid sister. "It's not often I get to see a pretty girl when I'm sitting out there with my fishing rod."

"Looks like you're throwing me a leer." I patted my face. "If I'd known how good this bruise would look, I'd have painted it on sooner."

This time, he did leer. "On you, anything looks good."

Back when I was thirteen, I'd have been tickled if Bill flirted with me. But I wasn't thirteen, and there was definitely something creepy about this whole scene.

Chapter Eight

By Tuesday, I had endured the hospital for as long as I could. Every time I fell asleep, I saw a huge black truck bearing down on me. Was that what happened? I couldn't tell. Would I ever know?

To distract myself, I conjugated French verbs, hoping to sleep better, but my eyes stayed open until sunlight brightened the narrow white slats at the window. If Bear had been there with me, I would have rested, but he was loafing around at Jake O'Toole's house, suffering the indignity of having to kowtow to a cat named Millicent. I made up my mind to call Mary Prescott as soon as I thought she'd had her first cup of coffee and ask her to come and get me. Another night of no sleep for fear of nightmares would push me right over the edge.

I was supposed to ring for a nurse to help me out of bed, but I managed to wobble across the cool tile floor to the bathroom and pee all by myself. Then I risked a glance in the mirror.

If anything, I looked worse than I had the day before. One side of my face was still swollen and purple; the other had turned a sickly yellow and green. I wondered if my damaged liver was changing as quickly, if it would fully recover, and what would happen if it didn't. So far, the doctor said it was too soon to know, but since I was healthy, she was hopeful.

I found myself clinging to that hope like a barnacle on the bottom of a boat.

Halfway back to my bed, the phone started to ring. I hobbled faster. It was my friend Janice, an actress in her native Haiti, and the volunteer manager for the Viva! theater. "Hon," she said the minute I picked up the phone, "I swear a person can't trust you out of her sight. What *are* you doing over there?" In my head I saw her tugging on a strand of curly black hair and deepening the worry lines in her wide brown forehead. "Why didn't you call me?"

I tried to think of something funny to say, but what came out was more like a sob. For a minute I couldn't speak.

"Talk to me, Heather. Are you all right?"

"Yes." Tears made the room swim. "But I just saw myself in the mirror. You'd cry, too, if you looked like your parents had been parrots."

"Oh, hon."

"Worse yet, my audition is supposed to be today. Our dear director will say he regrets that I can't be there. But now he won't even have to pretend to consider me. He'll be tickled to give the role to Victoria." In a way, I didn't blame him. Ms. Perfect had never once stood on the stage with her mouth gaping like a fish out of water.

"This is merely a tiny little speed bump on your road to stardom, hon," Janice said. "*The Tempest* is next, and you are perfect for Arielle."

I let her words sink into my soul, where it started to soothe the hurts. When we hung up, I lay there, missing her and the theater, letting tears run down into the pillow. I told myself to snap out of it and called Mary.

"Jake and Sam are working out a plan to keep the cabin under surveillance," she said. "I'll come and get you as soon as they have everything ready."

I caught my breath. "Surveillance?" Could I be bringing a threat to her cabin? I hadn't thought of that. I'd only been concerned about myself, and getting sprung from the hospital. "I can't do that to you."

Mary remained calm and firm. "No worries. It's just a precaution. My father was a detective and I'm used to stuff like that. I want you to come. I'm dying for adult conversation."

Longing with all my heart to believe her, I agreed.

Alicia Mendosa, the doctor, came in and went over my discharge orders, said I should see her in her office in two days, and wished me well.

Then I waited while the sun rose in the sky, my room got hotter and hotter, and I began to think I would be faced with another hospital lunch, bright cubes of jellied fruit juice and beef broth with a few parsley flakes floating on top, no doubt.

But Mary arrived, and full of instructions, Jake showed up two seconds later. Stern as a Baptist preacher, he stood with one hand on the bed rail and glared down at me from his lanky height. Mary sat in Angel's chair beside the bed, chewing a fingernail.

"When you remember what happened, call me," Jake said. "Tell *me* what comes back. Tell *only* me."

"Okay. I wear the tracer. I call you for permission to leave Sam's Resort, and I don't go anywhere, even to the doctor's office, without a deputy to escort me. I tell no one about what happened to me or what I saw. *If* I remember. Not even Mary."

"Correct."

"It sounds like you haven't told her any details about what she's getting into. That's not fair. You're not letting her make an informed decision."

Mary rose to her full five feet, one-inch height. "So, Jake, I can keep a secret. I used to go on stakeouts with Dad." I heard the tapping of her toe on the pale beige floor.

"Ah, women," Jake shot back, mouth twisted into a reluctant grin. "I keep forgetting how much you ladies like to work things around to your point of view." He handed me a small brown envelope, then turned for the door. "That's your tracer. Put it on. Now."

"Men," Mary said. "They really do come from a different planet."

"This isn't right. You should know everything that's going on. I can't do this to you."

"Sam is my cousin and I trust him, and I trust Jake. They will keep you safe, and I'm happy to help. My dad always said keeping the law is up to all of us. He said if we didn't, we'd all be up to our necks in crooks." She patted my shoulder. "Come on. Stop worrying. It's a lot nicer out at the cabin. Let's get going."

I told myself I'd only stay for a day or two. I opened Jake's envelope. Inside, I found an oval gold locket on a gold chain. It popped open to show a photo of Bear.

Mary took it and turned it over a couple of times. "Pretty fancy for Sterling County. Wonder where he got it." She fastened it around my neck. "One thing's for sure, no one will have a clue what it really is." She grabbed my duffel and started toward the door. "Got everything? I'll drive up to the entrance."

Like a tortoise, I followed, but a nurse came in

with a wheelchair and insisted that I sit in it. When he wheeled me out, I looked over my shoulder, as if I were leaving something important behind. The cardiac monitor, now silent and still, the plastic pitcher, the rumpled bed—eerie, empty.

Like my memory.

Angel Orlando waited in the hall. "I'm to follow you home." He stood aside for us to go ahead of him.

By the time I climbed into Mary's car, my knees shook. My heart thudded against my ribs. Rivulets of perspiration ran down my back and soaked into the rib belt that hugged me like a corset. I lowered myself gingerly onto the seat. As if I were one of her kids, Mary helped get me belted in.

While she drove along the lake, I worried. Mary reached over and touched my hand. "You probably aren't very comfortable." She was right. Even in the big luxury sedan she drove, at every bump, it felt as if someone shoved a dagger under my shoulder blade.

But that was nothing. Something terrible had happened to the quaint vacation community I loved. First, a body had turned up in the orchard above Sam's resort. Then, according to Jake, I'd witnessed a crime, and it must have been a big one because he thought someone had tried to kill me. Now, this Mariella person was missing.

The gravel driveway into Sam's Resort, shaded by towering pines, winds down to the big, old, half-timbered house known as the inn, although it is actually Sam and Penny's house. Just seeing it nestled there between the trees and the lake, quiet and peaceful, made me feel like I could breathe again. Mary stopped at the tiny parking lot behind the inn.

Angel got out of the police car and came to my window. "You're in good hands now. I'll be out in a couple of days to escort you to your doctor's appointment." With one of those gorgeous smiles, he stepped back. Too bad he was engaged to Doctor Mendosa.

Mary drove on and parked the car at the side of her cabin, a low blue-gray bungalow, one of seven set around the perimeter of Sam's big green lawn, which sloped down to the water. Travis and Jordan were instantly at the car, dripping from a plunge in the lake. They took my bag and after arguing about which of them would carry it, pounded up the stairs to the deck, each holding one strap. I plodded behind, holding the handrail for support.

There was a wide deck, and then a screened-in porch. Both went all the way across the front of the cabin. A picnic table and several lounge chairs occupied the deck. The screen door squeaked as Jordan yanked it open. He held it so I could enter. Inside the screened porch, a set of bunk beds stood against the wall on the right; on the left, a long table with an assortment of garage-sale chairs, a red and white checkered cloth, and a bouquet of wildflowers.

The door banged shut behind us. Jordan waved a hand at the bunks. "Travis and me sleep out here, so you can have the back bedroom. That's where the ghost is." With a big grin, he started inside. "Just kidding."

The main part of the cabin was one big room, with the kitchen at the back. A woman gathered the trash from under the sink. Her brown hair was pulled back off her suntanned face in a ponytail, and she wore Sam's uniform: navy shorts and a white shirt with

Sam's logo on the pocket. Mary introduced her as Jeannie.

"Sorry," Jeannie said. "I'm behind today. And I usually clean your sinks and vacuum every other day, but since Mariella ran off again, I don't have time to do it that often."

"You think she ran off?" Mary and I sounded like a chorus. "Again?"

"She did it last year, and the other day she was all gaga about some hunk from California who helped her change her tire in the pouring rain. I don't know why the sheriff thinks something bad has happened. She'll be back as soon as he gets tired of her mouth."

"Just wait until her boyfriend finds out she's gone," Jordan said.

Jeannie snorted. "Yeah, Charlie. He'll kill her."

****

Just as Mary promised, things were infinitely better at the cabin. Even the air smelled good. It had blown over clean sweeps of snow in the high Cascades then swooped down to pick up the scent of mown grass. Every summer I could remember smelled just like that.

Mary was in the kitchen making raspberry pie, so I spread a towel on a chaise lounge on the deck and nestled into the soft cushion, thankful to rest in the sunshine that filtered down through an old pear tree. I wanted to ask Jordan and Travis what they knew about Mariella and if they knew who Charlie was, but they had run right back down to the lake. Along with a bunch of other kids, they were on the dock, tucking their legs up and hugging their knees as they jumped off, climbing out, and doing it again.

I must have fallen asleep and didn't move until

Bear's damp muzzle nudged my hand a couple of hours later. Jake stood by the screen door, holding it open as Jordan came out of the cabin, carrying a bowl filled to the brim with water. "Here, Bear." A smile lit Jordy's face. He looked like a slightly damp angel.

I slept again until the rich aroma of garlic, tomatoes, and herbs wafted out through the screens and swirled around me. I struggled to my feet.

"Mom!" Jordan bounded up onto the deck. He ran to the screen door, flung it open, and pelted into the cabin yelling, "Mom, there's some guy here who says you used to teach him in fifth grade. I told him to come on up."

The door banged shut behind him, and I turned to face Mary's former student. I'd expected a kid, but the man coming up the stairs had been in fifth grade about the same time I had. Baggy shorts and a loose T-shirt with faded rock stars hid his body. Reflective sunglasses shielded his eyes. Long blond hair blew around his face and tangled with his diamond earring.

As he mounted the last stair, he extended his hand. "I'm Matt McCrae, and I know you're not Mrs. Prescott." His smile made dimples in each cheek.

I had a déjà vu moment, one of those funky sensations that I had met him before. His hand, firm and warm, engulfed mine. Bear pushed his black bulk in between us, as if he thought he needed to protect me. Matt McCrae slowly released my hand.

The screen door openned with a squeak. "My gosh," Mary said. "If I hadn't heard you say your name, I would never have recognized you. You used to be shorter than me."

He chuckled—a rich, happy chortle. "My family

camped at the county park every summer back then," he said. "Remember? Sis and I used to walk over here and hang out because you made such great pies."

"Of course." Mary grinned. "I still make great pies, and I've never figured out how to cook a little spaghetti. Can you stay for dinner?"

Again, the dimples. "Tell me what I can do to help." Before he followed Mary into the cabin, he took off his sunglasses and gazed at me for a long moment, his blue eyes sober. The color startled me. I'd expected them to be hazel. I'd met, or seen, Matt McCrae before.

But where? When? Why didn't he remind me?

I went in to set the table and to eavesdrop on their conversation. Matt stood beside the kitchen sink, tearing lettuce and dropping it into the salad bowl, as if he did this every day. He said, "I know Mom still works on fund raisers for the school."

"She does." Mary sounded perfectly at ease. She shook an admonishing cucumber at him. "And she's kept me well informed."

While everyone found a seat, Mary brought a huge round pasta bowl heaped with spaghetti and thick red sauce to the table in the screened porch. "The funny thing is, your mother doesn't seem to know exactly what you do now, Matt."

He looked amused. "Oh, I work at a big gray desk in a big gray building. Along with hundreds of other ants, I crawl in and out of the colony every day."

Mary raised her eyebrows. "In high school, you blew up the chem lab more times than anyone in the history of the school. And I know you had a scholarship to MIT, so how come I don't believe you ended up with a dull job?"

"Oh, I'm still interested in chemistry. I just don't blow everything up." He grinned at the boys. "Hey, do you guys like to water ski?"

Jordan shot a glance at his mother. "Yeah, but Mom never goes fast enough."

Matt's mouth curved in a suppressed grin. "My mom always acted like she was driving her station wagon to the grocery store."

"Exactly," Jordan murmured, ducking his head.

"If it's okay with Mrs. Prescott, I'll take you out after dinner."

"Sure, but you have to stop calling me Mrs. Prescott if you want a piece of pie when you come back in. And you two need to clear the table first."

Right then, Jake O'Toole showed up, carrying a half-full sack of dog food.

Jake shook Matt's hand. "Dave. Nice to see you."

Dave, not Matt. Really?

"That your boat out there at the end of the fuel dock?"

I turned to look. My heart stopped cold. I was beginning to believe some of my nightmares were real, and somewhere in my nightmares, there was a boat that looked a lot like that one.

Chapter Nine

Darn Matt McCrae. His smile got me every time.
Those dimples and the sparkly light in his bright blue
eyes drew me right in and made me smile back.
Everybody knows that smiling elevates your heart and
makes the whole world look better. And that makes you
like the person who made you smile in the first place.
Even if you're not sure you want to like them, or if you
should like them, or what might happen if you do.

Mary explained that although he was nicknamed
Matt after his favorite uncle, his real name was David
Matthew, so it made sense to her that the sheriff might
call him Dave. But there was something fishy about
him. Who the heck was he, and what was he up to?

Sam's Resort was a quiet family place, not a meat
market to find a new girlfriend, so why would he stay
all by himself in the big old house? It was known as
Sam's Inn, but really, it had only a couple of attic
bedrooms to rent. Sam and Penny lived downstairs.

From the deck of Mary's cabin, I had a bird's view
of everything that went on at Sam's. Guys who were on
vacation drank beer. They swam in the lake or fell
asleep by the pool and burned to a crisp, bright red.
Matt did not. Matt or Dave, whoever he was, acted like
a man on a mission. I'd been watching for three full
days, and as far as I could tell, he spent his time in
Sam's attic, which had to be as hot and stuffy as a gym

locker. The only time he showed up was in the evening, when he took the boys water skiing. And he claimed to be on vacation.

The screen door squeaked and Mary came out onto the deck, a paperback novel in one hand, a glass of iced tea in the other. "Ready?" she asked. We headed across the lawn toward the dock. Shadows were stretching long across the soft green grass, which felt cool, dampened with early dew. Mary said, "Bill Harlan phoned a little while ago, while you were in the shower. He said he stopped by to see you this afternoon, but we were gone. It must have been when I took you to see the doctor."

"I'm surprised. I've never been anything to him but Tom's bratty little sister."

Mary raised a brow as if she didn't quite believe that. "I heard he spends a lot of time at the casino since it opened. There's a rumor that he lost a bundle—blew right through his inheritance." She shot me a glance, questioning, as if I might know all about it.

"I have no clue."

"It's odd. He never seems short of money."

"Maybe he hit a winning streak."

"Anyway, he seems anxious about your memory."

I could tell by her tone that she was leading up to something, and I wished she'd just say what she was thinking. I tried to brush it off. "Oh, Bill is just Bill."

She offered another questioning glance and said, "I wonder if his marriage is all that solid. He acts as if he's sweet on you."

I cringed. "I hope you don't think I'd be open to a liaison with him. We have never even been friends." I'd heard enough about Bill and needed to change the subject. "Seriously, he's only a neighbor."

At the sandy beach next to the dock, Mary turned a couple of lounge chairs to face the lake and plopped into one. I eased myself down and brought my feet up slowly, one at a time, holding my breath to keep my ribs steady. "I feel older than God's grandma."

Mary laughed. "As long as you don't look it."

She waved at Jordan, who was sitting on the end of the dock with water skis on, looking over his shoulder to see if we were watching. A little way off the dock, Matt stood in his boat, coiling the tow rope. I felt certain I'd seen him before he showed up at Mary's cabin, and that he was connected to what had happened to me before I ended up in the hospital. Either that, or I was going crazy.

There was no way I'd ask him. After all the warnings from Sheriff O'Toole, I wasn't about to ask anyone anything, no matter how much I longed to know. Seriously, a person could drive herself right around the bend worrying.

I'd rather think about Angel Orlando, who had followed Mary's car to and from Dr. Alicia Mendosa's office. Even if he and Alicia were engaged, the man was worth a second thought, maybe a third. He sat beside me in the waiting room, and when he smiled, worries vanished. Okay, enough already. If there was one thing I'd learned from Alex St. John, it was that handsome men were heartbreakers.

Long slanting rays danced on the rippled surface of the water. It was a lovely time of day, a quiet, reflective time. Behind us in the cabins, families were getting out game boards as after-dinner coffee brewed, and parents were herding little ones off to their baths.

Sam sauntered down the dock and squatted beside Jordy. Jordan nodded a couple of times. In the boat, Travis played out the towrope while Matt motored slowly away. Jordy raised one thumb, the motor roared, and as the echoes bounced off the hills behind us, he flew away on the skis.

In the chair beside mine, Mary sat up straight; smiling and proud. "Good job!"

The boat raced across the lake, swung in a wide arc, and after a few minutes, turned back toward us. I had a clear view of Jordan's square chest and shoulders, childish, but struggling toward manhood. "Look how he's crossing the wake," Mary crowed. Jordan wobbled, tried to stay up, but plunged sideways into the water.

It was one of my nightmares: a boat racing toward me, a skier falling as he stretched his arm out over the water, and then a boat that looked like Matt's bearing down on him. My heart pounded. I couldn't get enough air. I gripped the arms of my chair, closed my eyes, and prayed. It wasn't a nightmare. I'd actually seen it. And it was happening again.

Mary put her hand on my arm. "You've gone totally white. What's wrong?"

Jordy popped to the surface, laughing and shaking big drops of water out of his coppery hair. He stretched out in an adequate crawl and swam to the dock, and I could breathe again. Travis picked up the skis, and Matt motored slowly back in. It was Travis's turn.

I couldn't wait. I went up to the cabin and phoned Jake O'Toole. I expected him to sound relieved, maybe even excited, that my memory was coming back. I thought he'd be eager—that he'd want to come right out and talk to me. Instead, he sounded tired, weary.

I started to wonder if I was wrong, if my brain was so damaged that I was hopelessly confused, and he just didn't want to be the one to tell me. Practically begging him to agree, I said, "I thought it was a nightmare, but now I know it's real."

"What else do you remember?"

Remember. He said *remember*. I wasn't confused. It wasn't merely a bad dream. It was a memory that had been hiding in my subconscious mind, trying to get out. "That's all, but it means my other nightmares must be real, too. At least some of them."

"Keep them under your hat until I have a chance to get out there."

"When?"

"You'll see me when I get there."

That rocked me back on my heels. Something was wrong. I spent the rest of the evening wondering what it was. That night, every time I closed my eyes, I saw Jordy fall again, only it wasn't Jordy at all. Turning in my narrow bed, trying to sleep, turning again, bunching my pillow under my head first one way and then another, I saw it over and over—the black silhouette of a water-skier tumbling into the water. I heard the sound of breaking bone as the men in the boat clubbed the water-skier.

I was wide awake. It really did happen. Some of my other nightmares had to be just as real. But no matter how hard I gritted my teeth and concentrated, I could not bring more to light in my conscious mind.

When I heard the boys clunk their cereal bowls onto the table in the kitchen, I got right out of bed. I had to talk to someone. Maybe I couldn't tell them anything, but I could ask what they knew about this

Mariella, and I did, even before I got the coffee started.

Jordy began, "Well, see, after we found you last Friday, Mom made us sit at the table in the porch because we went away from Sam's without permission. She always does that for the big lectures, but we never got the lecture because Sam came over right then and said had we seen Mariella."

"Yeah," Travis interrupted. "Sam said she didn't come home the night before, so Aunt Mary shooed us outside, like we shouldn't hear about somebody having sex and not coming home. But she shouldn't have done that because we know stuff, like we know all about Mariella's boyfriends."

"Yup," Jordy said. "She was lying on the dock with Jeannie, see. That's her friend. Me and Travis were snorkeling around, and we heard everything."

"Not on purpose," Travis said with a grin.

"No, accidental," Jordy added, eyes sparkling. "Anyway, Mariella's all, like, 'He's so cool and he's got a really cool sports car, and I'll never meet anyone like him again. I'll probably cry all night, Jeannie. He could have had the decency to tell me if he didn't want to go out anymore.' And then Jeannie said, 'You're crazy, Mariella. Charlie dumped you here and took off, but he'll be back. He beat you up for dancing with that guy at the rodeo. And he practically killed the guy. What do you think he'll do if he finds out about Ken?'"

Jordan pulled in a breath. "We could of told Sheriff O'Toole right away, but oh, no, we're just children, so we got shooed outside. Anyway, after we were snorkeling, Mariella took off in her rusty beater car and never came back."

"Do you know Charlie?" I asked.

"We've seen him," Jordy said, nodding. "Last year and the year before."

"He's a motorcycle dude," Travis added. "And he's got a gang."

My brain was racing. I had never seen or heard of Charlie, but our cabin was farther up-lake and our area was less populated, so that wasn't surprising. "Does Charlie live around here?"

Jordy shrugged. "He kind of travels around with his gang. I bet he came back and made Mariella go with him."

Or beat her up and killed her. I shuddered.

The boys were on their feet, bending over to put their bowls down for Bear. He slurped at the milk and cereal, happily swishing his tail on the floor. Jordan fixed his big hazel eyes on me. "Mom said maybe we could get a little dog, but I want one like Bear. You'll help me convince her, won't you Heather?" His hair stood up in wisps above his forehead, shining in the sunlight like a polished copper crown. He looked like a poster child for an expensive brand of vitamins.

I couldn't imagine the strength of will it would take to say no. "I'll see what I can do." I felt a little sorry for ganging up on Mary, but the truth was, a kid like Jordan needed a dog like Bear.

"Thanks." He rewarded me with a grin, picked up the cereal bowls, and put them in the sink. "Time to go fishing."

The screen door had barely squeaked shut behind them when the phone rang. Jake at last! But it wasn't Jake on the phone.

"Good morning, sunshine."

I had convinced myself I was over Alex, but when

I heard his voice, my heart lurched.

"Please tell me you're not going to leave me standing on your doorstep again."

"I wouldn't do that. I'm not that awful." Smooth, Heather. Witty, too.

"You did. You ran away and I hung out on your porch until your favorite Thai takeout got cold. After I went to bat for you and got you that audition."

"Okay, I did." Too bad. After all, he had dumped me. And I thought I'd gotten the audition on my own. Regardless, if this phone call meant that he was crawling back now, I wasn't interested. No matter how many times I had dreamed of getting back together.

"You didn't even show up at auditions. So, tell me what happened." Below the bantering tone, Alex's voice carried an undercurrent of concern.

My heart started to soften, but I didn't want to go there—okay, I was afraid to go there. "What are you complaining about?" I asked. "Isn't Victoria there, practicing day and night to be your leading lady?"

For a moment, he didn't respond. Then he said, "Look, why don't we start at the beginning? Janice told me you were hurt in a hit and run, and I'm sorry. Besides that, I'm worried. She said you're pretty beat up and you've lost your memory. What's the story?"

"The first time Janice called, I was a little spacey. Actually, very spacey, but now the only problem is, I can't remember anything about a couple of days." I crossed my fingers. My Catholic upbringing didn't allow for lying.

"You remember running away from me?"

"I had to get away so I could think."

"Heather."

The way he said my name turned my knees to jelly. Face it. I'm worse than Pavlov's dog.

"You are beautiful and talented and funny, and I'm attracted to you more than I like to admit, but the idea of committing to one person for the rest of my life makes me claustrophobic."

Although I tried hard, I couldn't think of a glib reply.

"You hear what I'm saying?"

I sighed. "Look, we had some great times together. But I have huge issues to worry about right now, and I can't even think about you in a romantic way." I said goodbye and hung up.

By the time I was well, *Taming of the Shrew* would be ready to open. Alex and Victoria would play the leading roles. And, almost certainly, dear director Donovan would invite me to be Victoria's understudy—again. Was I crazy to hope she might come down with the plague? Just in case, I went to the bedroom and got my script. It could happen, and I had nothing else to do but wait for Jake.

Chapter Ten

By noon, Jake still hadn't arrived. If my returning memory was so damn important, where was he? After lunch, Mary sent Travis and Jordan off to pick berries, and she headed down to the pool. Half an hour later, the boys came back. Red-faced, sweating, without their berry buckets, they pounded up the steps to the deck.

Travis said, "Heather, you won't believe it."

Jordy horned in. "Oh man, we've got to call the sheriff. It's too weird, man." He jerked open the screen door and they raced into the cabin.

I followed them.

Jordy grabbed the phone and dialed, then asked to speak to Sheriff O'Toole. He rubbed a hand across his forehead, leaving a muddy smudge. "Can he call me back? Well, yeah, it's important. Like, real important. Tell him Travis and me found something."

I poured cold lemonade for them. "What? Where?"

"Mariella's car," Jordy said.

My heart stopped. "Is she in it?"

"No."

They each grabbed a glass, took a long drink, and headed for the porch, both talking at once, describing Mariella's old, battered, shattered, black car. In less than five minutes, Matt ran up the stairs onto the deck. He wore tight jeans and a buttoned white shirt, and his hair was back in a ponytail. No earring. No sloppy T-shirt or baggy shorts. Hazel eyes, I realized with a start. Not blue. He looked like Dave. He *was* Dave, the scuba diver. For a moment, my mouth hung open.

Dave or Matt, whoever, opened the screen door and stepped into the porch. "I hear you guys found something."

The boys started over.

Mary chose that moment to come back from the pool. "Why aren't you and Travis picking . . .?" Mary looked them up and down. "What's wrong?"

Arms folded, Matt leaned against the door frame.

Mary stared at him for a moment, then went to the table and sat down. She beckoned the boys to sit beside her and curved an arm around each. "Tell me."

Travis sighed. I saw the tension ease out of his shoulders. "Okay. We were on our way up the hill to Vandenberg's to pick berries."

Jordan broke in, "Yeah. Do you know where they live, Matt?"

"Not exactly."

Travis pointed toward the hills behind the cabin. "If you take the short cut, it's right up there behind Sam's orchard."

"Gotcha."

"We climb up the cliff. It's not a cliff, really." Jordan held up a freckled arm at a sharp angle. "But steep, like this. You have to grab onto bushes so you don't slide back down."

Matt nodded. "I think I know where."

"So, I'm racing Travis and we're going as fast as we can, and about half-way up, there's this flat spot, kind of. It's pretty big." Jordan spaced his hands wide apart. "There's some old campfires. Teenagers hike up there and smoke dope and, you know. . .."

"Make out?"

"Yeah." They both nodded, and Travis continued, "That's where we found Mariella's old black bug."

Jordy nodded. "It must of tumbled down from the top. It's altogether crumpled up and the windows are all broken out."

For once, Mary didn't correct his grammar. She looked from one to the other, frowning with concern. "Are you sure it's hers? Could it be a different car?"

"Mom, if you'd been there, you'd know. There's junk all over inside. Like, she always had hamburger sacks and giant soft drink cups and stuff. It's hers."

"We didn't get too close at first," Travis said.

"Yeah, but then we peeked in—you know, to see if she was inside."

Mary and I exchanged a long look. I turned to Matt. His eyes met and held mine. "I'd better go see," he said. "Mary, is it okay if they show me?"

"Hey! We called Sheriff O'Toole." Jordy stared at him. "So how come you showed up?"

"I've been working with Sheriff O'Toole a bit."

A tiny part of me rejoiced, in spite of the grimness of the boys' news, hearing Matt confirm that Mary was right—that he was on the right side of the law.

Mary, who had never doubted it, said, "I want to talk to the boys for a couple of minutes." She chewed a fingernail, looking worried. For the kids? About Matt? What?

Matt told the boys to wait right there with Mary. "I'll be back in a few."

He hurried off, following the service road behind the cabins. A few minutes later, wearing his cargo shorts and T-shirt, his hair flowing loosely to his shoulders, he strolled back across the lawn in front of the cabins, as if he had not a care anywhere. His eyes were blue again. He didn't even look like the same person. So, why the disguise?

He and the boys hiked up the hill behind the cabin, leaving Mary and me to speculate. Mary said, "If Mariella merely went off with Charlie, why would her car be wrecked and abandoned?"

"Exactly. And if she isn't in her car, where is she?"

"Charlie must have come back, just as Jeannie predicted, and beaten her. Maybe he didn't intend to kill her, but she died."

I nodded. "Then he made it look as if she had accidentally gone off the road and fallen out of her car as it rolled down the hill." You don't get to pick when and how you're going to die. The idea settled in the pit of my stomach like a lump of lead.

"That means her body is lying somewhere on the hillside," Mary said.

"As I was until Jordy and Travis found me." I was so lucky. I was supposed to be dead, too. "But why would Charlie want to kill me?"

"That's clear. For some reason, he thought you knew something."

When they came back, Matt looked grim. "Stay here, guys," he said, "and don't talk to anyone about this. I'll be back as soon as I verify the registration on the car."

Mary couldn't stop chewing her fingernails. The boys sat in the porch and played Uno with her, quietly for a change. I took a bunch of deep breaths, did a couple of yoga poses, and when none of that helped, I got out my script and tried to focus on it.

Finally, just before dinner, Matt returned. "We're going to have to get a search party out," he said, "and Jake wants to talk to the boys. Are you okay with me taking them to see him?"

By the time Jordy and Travis returned, the sun's long evening rays had chased the shadow of the pear tree all the way across Mary's deck. The boys were tired and flushed with the heat that boiled up off the town's asphalt streets, but stuffed with pizza.

Mary put the dinner she had prepared for them in the refrigerator. She wanted to talk to them while she cleaned up the kitchen, so I took a handful of chocolate sandwich cookies and a glass of red wine—the doctor had forbidden wine, actually, but it was a teeny, tiny glass—outside to the deck.

I watched wispy clouds turn pink, and then purple and gold as the light faded, and thought about my sister. I'd always known that ever since Harmony died, Mom had been terrified that something would happen to Tom and me. Suddenly, I had a better grasp of what that meant and how deep her fear went, and I started to forgive her for being angry with me and blaming me for not saving Harmony. As that hard, cold knot in my heart unraveled a bit, tears rolled down my cheeks, and I started to forgive myself for not preventing Harmony from flying off the trampoline.

I was halfway through my wine when I saw Matt sauntering over from Sam's house in his baggy shorts. I dried my eyes and blew my nose. Slowly, he climbed the steps to the deck. He paused and looked at me for a long moment before he asked, "May I join you?"

When I nodded, he settled into the chaise beside

mine. He looked tired and worried enough to tug at my heart strings. I reminded myself not to fall under the spell that comes from sharing the most magical time of day. This man had secrets. He had not been straightforward with me. I waited for him to speak first, and for what seemed like a very long time, we sat in silence.

He slid his hand over and stole my last cookie from the plate on my lap. "I've wondered if I'd ever have a chance to meet you," he said. His arm brushed mine, very lightly, and electricity shot right through my body.

Instantly, I wanted him to touch me until every square inch of my skin felt alive and glowing and treasured. I caught my breath. I had to wait until my pulse slowed a bit, until I could speak again. "Why?"

"I'd like to know you." He smiled, and although his dimples looked as charming as ever, I did not smile back. He broke the cookie in half and held one piece in front of my mouth. It was hard enough to stay aloof when we were sitting side by side looking at the first evening star, pretending we were not acutely aware of each other; impossible if we shared a cookie. If his fingertips touched my lips, even accidentally, I'd be done for.

I waved temptation away with my hand. "You eat it." More than anything, I wanted the truth. "You've been pretending you're here on vacation. But you're not. And I have a feeling that you've been spying on me. Who *are* you?"

He chewed slowly, staring at the lake. Finally, he responded, "It's important that I look like any other guest here at Sam's. After this afternoon, you probably realize that I'm here because of my job. But don't make the mistake of mixing up my job—and no, I'm not going to tell you what that is—with me."

I frowned. What was *that* supposed to mean?

After a moment he said, "Personally, I live in Seattle, in the Fremont neighborhood, and I've had season tickets at Viva! for the last three years. I haven't missed a single play, so I've seen every one you've had a role in, and I've wanted to meet you. I've actually tried to get up the nerve to send a note backstage to ask if you would like to have a drink with me."

I smiled in spite of myself. Getting a note like that from a fan would have been fun and exciting. "You're kidding."

"Nope. I'm the guy who jumps up and yells 'Brava' every time the beautiful Heather Shelton steps onto the stage. Even if you were the ugly step-mother."

I loved the ugly step-mother role from last year's version of *Cinderella*. If he had offered me half of his cookie right then, I'd have taken it.

"Sometimes you're dressed in black and move the sets around at intermission. Haven't you ever wondered who was applauding?"

"What I wonder is who's sitting beside you." Not that it matters, I told myself.

"Oh, my mom, my sister. Anyone who's too soft-hearted to watch me trudge off the theater by myself."

I laughed at the image this created in my mind; then saw a flash of triumph in his eyes, as if he'd said "Gotcha."

Instantly, my defenses came back up. All he would need was a few minutes studying theater posters to learn that much about me. And a phone call to anyone at Viva! could have reaped tons of information. "You could have learned about my work at the theater without ever stepping inside Viva!'s door."

"My interest in you is genuine." He slid an arm around my shoulders. "I can prove it."

Confusion and loneliness disappeared as his lips touched mine. My heart, which has no sense at all, opened to his warmth. I melted into his embrace, forgetting everything. The safety of his arms welcomed me. I wanted him to keep me there.

He pushed my hair back behind my ear, slowly and gently. With his fingers lingering lightly on my neck, he kissed the tip of my ear. "I shouldn't have done that." He pulled away.

Like icy cold water, his words splashed over me.

Behind us, the screen door squeaked and we both turned to look over our shoulders.

Jordan stood in the doorway, framed in light from the porch. He looked scrubbed clean of the afternoon's dirt and his hair lay close to his head, shiny and wet. "Hey, Matt, you want some hot chocolate?"

"Thanks, but I'd better go."

"I thought you were going to play poker with us."

Matt stood up. He kissed the tip of his finger, then touched it to the end of my nose before he started across the deck to the stairs. "Another time, huh? Why don't you see if you can beat Heather?"

****

The next morning, I was up before the boys. It had been another sleepless night, and my eyes felt as dry and scratchy as if they'd sprouted barnacles. Red, rimmed with dark shadows, they topped off the yellow-green bruises around my cheekbones. I looked worse than I had the day before, but I was too tired to care.

Mary snored softly as I tiptoed past her open door in my swim suit. Bear and I crossed the porch and we walked across the cool wet grass together. At the pool, I laid my towel on a chair beside the hot tub and stuck my feet in the water. At first it felt too hot, but after a few seconds, I eased on in, ready for a quiet soak. Leaning my head back on the rim, I closed my eyes.

Not two minutes later, a familiar voice asked, "May I join you?"

Instantly off balance, I looked up. "Haven't we just had this conversation?"

Matt sat down and dangled his legs in the water. "I don't think we finished it. And before anything else happens, . . ." He slipped into the water. "I enjoyed kissing you last night. Very much."

"I'm a sucker for nice kisses."

"There's a big red-lettered 'but' in your voice."

No duh. "You lied to me and to Mary."

"Lied? When?"

I could hardly believe my ears. I glared at him. I'd spent half the night wanting him, all the while feeling that I couldn't trust him. "You said you came over just to say hi to your old teacher. Now, tell me. Was that a crock of bull or what?"

"I didn't lie to you. I left some parts to your imagination, but I didn't say anything that wasn't true."

A couple of women had spread their towels on lounge chairs by the swimming pool and were rubbing that sunscreen that smells like coconuts on their arms and legs, settling in for a morning of tanning and chatting. In a place where hardly anything happens, Matt and I were obvious gossip fodder.

I lowered my voice and turned to face him. "You

left a great deal to the imagination." I wanted to scream and throw things at him, but I settled for ticking his crimes off on my fingers. "First of all, you disguised yourself. Secondly, you pretended that your purpose in coming to Mary's cabin was to see your old teacher. Third, you said your friend had bailed out and left you alone on vacation. Fourth, you let on that you work at a boring desk job, but you're sneaking around here like a double agent. Fifth, you kissed me and said you shouldn't have, and now you say you enjoyed it."

Tears tried to form in the corners of my eyes. My throat constricted and my voice quavered. I wanted to feel safe again, and warm, and cherished, the way I did that tiny moment when he held me.

But his eyes looked hard and closed. "I think you made some inaccurate assumptions."

I just stared at him. "I don't believe this. You deliberately misled me and now you're blaming me for misunderstanding."

He set his jaw, square and determined. "Listen. Here's the truth. I don't do much field work. Part of the reason I'm involved in this project is that I have roots and connections here, including my acquaintance with Mary. Most of the time, I work in the chem lab or sit at my desk and like Hercule Poirot, exercise my little gray cells." As he tapped his forehead with his finger, the frown lines disappeared and a hint of smile tugged briefly at the corners of his lips.

"Can you explain why you said your friend didn't show up?"

"I suppose I could tell you that he was an associate rather than a friend." He rubbed a hand across his face, wiping away perspiration. "I agree that I stretched the truth on that point. Regardless, I was supposed to meet him here and he didn't show up."

"*Was* an associate?" All the pieces clicked together, like the last few pieces in a jigsaw puzzle. "He didn't show up because he's dead."

Deep in my gut, I had a feeling that Matt's associate, whoever he was, happened to be Mariella's new boyfriend. "Charlie killed him for stealing his girl. And he killed her, too." I sucked in a breath. "Then, somehow, he found out I was at the cabin and was afraid I might talk, so he ran me down and left me for dead. That's why Jake insists that I be kept under surveillance." I shivered, wishing with all my heart I was wrong. I prayed that Mariella would show up soon.

Matt pushed himself up and sat on the edge of the tub, his legs still in the water. "I hoped there was another explanation when we didn't hear from him." Steam rose from his body into the clear morning air.

"So, you lied."

He sighed. "Next to that, my most despicable fault, I believe, is that I came here in disguise." He gazed out across the lake.

"Right." I looked at him. He had a good body, okay, better than good. Muscle definition all over the place, six-pack abs, everything. "You've been wearing deliberately sloppy clothes and glasses, letting your hair loose, and your eyes are blue. Sometimes you wear a great big diamond earring. But sometimes you look, and even sound completely different." When I said it, it sounded ridiculous.

He glanced down at me. "How about when you take a role at the theater? Aren't you setting out to deceive your audience—make them believe you are the character you're playing?" He slipped back into the water beside me.

My entire back tensed. I glared at him. "You're twisting everything around to avoid my issue."

"I'm not, Heather." A thread of anger edged the patience out of his tone. "I want you to see that my job is similar to yours. We both play a role when we go to work. I'm not Matt, private person, when I'm working. I'm Matt the spy, or Matt the chemical analyst, or Matt the low-profile snoop."

"When I play a role, everyone knows it. People come to be entertained, to engage in make believe." My agitation made my voice louder, and Matt held a finger to his lips.

I looked at our audience and they both appeared to be in deep concentration, poring over women's magazines, but I saw that one held hers upside down. "Look, we can't even have a private conversation. I'm going to go take a shower."

I got out of the hot tub. "I'm going to study the role of Katherina until I can say every line backwards, and I'm going pray to God that Victoria will come down with chicken pox and the doctor will let me drive back to Seattle."

I was certain the magazines had been lowered just enough for curious eyes to peek over the tops. And I will do anything Alex wants, even meaningless gratuitous sex, as long as he helps me onto the stage.

Matt got to the chair where I'd left my towel before I did. He picked it up and spread it open, as if to wrap it around me the way mothers do when their children are cold and tired. Not wanting to contribute further to the resort's news of the day, I obliged by turning my back.

Some treacherous part of me silently dared him to touch me. I kept myself straight to avoid leaning against him.

As he tucked it around my shoulders, he leaned close to my ear. "Ah, Kate. Sweet Kate."

"Stop making fun of me."

"Sorry. Let's go out on the dock for a minute. There's something I want to tell you."

Turning, I crossed my arms on my chest and frowned at him. Let him call me Kate. I'd rather be a shrew than a pushover.

"Please." His eyes had the puffy look of too little sleep. Clearly, I wasn't the only one lying awake at night. I couldn't help it. I softened. After all, I had the whole long day ahead of me, with nothing to do but rest my liver. What harm could it do to listen?

Our eyes made a silent agreement and without any more words, we walked out to the end, away from curious ears. We sat on the splintery dock with our backs to the sun. Not even Travis and Jordan were out there yet. Neither of us spoke. The shimmering blue lake rested, calm and serene. Sitting there reconnected me with the peace of earlier summers, long with tranquil days. I began to hear what he had been saying. I looked at him. He was leaning slightly forward, with his hands on the edge, gazing down into the water.

After a minute, he raised his head. "I understand your suspicions. You've been severely injured. You're under surveillance for your own protection. Those are good reasons." He didn't smile. In fact, he was frowning slightly. "I haven't explained what I'm doing here, and I'm not going to. Not yet." His gaze slid over my face and his tone softened. "Perhaps your heart has been injured, too."

I hadn't expected kindness. Tears pressed against my eyelids. I forced them back. "You said you wanted to tell me something."

He spoke slowly, as if choosing his words with care. "I'd like to try one more time to explain why I do what I do."

Inside, I felt a flutter of excitement: hope trying to undo the tight knot of fear in my chest. "Okay."

"When I was new to my job, I watched a training video made by Live Like King Tut, an exotic travel adventure company that treats guests like pharaohs while they ride around the desert on camels and sleep on Persian rugs in silk tents. Basically, all the employees, from camel drivers to tent attendants are on stage. When any member of the staff is on duty, regardless of any private frustrations or worries, he or she must act as if they are actually serving a deity." He looked at me, as if trying to decide whether to continue.

I nodded, wondering where the story would go.

"In the same way, my employer expects that I set aside my personal feelings and wishes and play a role. If I don't, important information may not be gathered, for example. In the worst case, lives could be lost."

I should stop acting like a pouting child. That's what he meant. And he was right. Sort of.

He continued, "Here at Sam's, I want to look like just another vacationer, laid back, slow moving, easy going. Well, okay, even sloppy. That way, I can walk around here as much as I want, and no one pays any attention to me. I see and hear everything that's going on because everyone just says hi and goes right back to whatever they were doing. Can you imagine what would happen if I showed up in a suit? Or in a shirt like

Jake's with a badge on it?"

"You're right. You'd be a hot topic. Everybody would be watching and talking about you. Lake Sterling mentality, Mary calls it."

He enveloped my hand in both of his and looked at me with an intensity that made the bottom fall out of my stomach. I couldn't have looked away if I tried. He kissed my forehead. "Here are some true statements. Number one, I am very sorry for any distress I've caused you. Number two, I do have season tickets to Viva!. I think it's a wonderful little theater." Sliding one hand up my arm, making me greedy for his touch, he leaned toward me. "And number three, I've wished I could meet you. That's not a lie." His hand cupped the back of my neck. His mouth hovered inches from mine, so close I could sense the warmth of his mouth.

I put a finger on his lips and looked into his eyes— blue, blue, blue, to die for blue, like the lake in early morning. Some perverse instinct made me want to push him away.

Chapter Eleven

Even before Matt joined me in the hot tub that morning, Jake had half a dozen men combing the hillside where Travis and Jordan found Mariella's car. Mary and I waited for news, thinking we'd hear something at any moment, something that would put our minds at ease, but the whole day went by without word of any kind. With each hour, my heart sank a little farther.

That evening, as the sky turned orange and gold, Matt came over and told us Jake had called off the search, that he was confident that Mariella was not there. Mary and I began to hope she had simply gone off somewhere, and that Charlie had wrecked her car in revenge.

I also hoped Matt would sit on the deck with me and share my chocolate sandwich cookies, but he didn't linger. I fell asleep that night remembering his kiss— and wondering why I'd pushed him away.

I had a dream about a petite young woman doing back flips on a high balance beam, wearing red shoes with incredibly high heels. The balance beam vanished and she froze in place, upside down, suspended in the air, red shoes pointed directly at me. Her smile grew to an enormous crimson fissure. It was her throat, slit from side to side, and filled with bright red blood. She beckoned me to come closer. I backed away, but her image came nearer, growing larger every second. It reached out, as if to engulf me.

I woke up gasping. As I bolted straight up in bed, pain stabbed through my chest from my broken ribs. I struggled to my feet and braced myself on the headboard, taking short, shallow breaths. Stupid. I was stupid. At last the pain subsided and I could stand upright. I sighed. I could blame no one but myself for my predicament.

Thunder cracked sharply overhead, then rolled across the sky, deep and resonant. A cold draft swept in. I shrugged into the bathrobe Mary had loaned me and groped my way to the hall, past Mary's room, and into the living room. I paused as lightning flashed in the big front windows and splashed patches of light across the floor. Immediately, the thunder came in great echoing billows.

In the following stillness, I heard the gentle purring of Mary's sleep, and as if someone had reached out and touched me, a current of fear and apprehension drained away. It was only a dream. Already, it had lost its power to make my heart pound and my breath come in gasps. I had to believe that eventually, this whole summer, including the nightmares and broken ribs, would fade like the lightning and drift away like the thunder.

I stole across the screened-in porch where the boys took turns sleeping in the top bunk, pressed my nose into the screen door, drew in its tinny smell, and looked out. Far across the lawn, past the other cabins, a weak yellow light shone from a fixture under the eaves of Sam's inn, but otherwise, everything looked black. A gust of ozone-laden wind drove droplets of rain in on my face, stinging and refreshing. I stepped back, pulled both sides of my robe across my chest, and anchored them there with folded arms.

I burrowed into the warmth, the way I did when my sister and I were small, sitting on Dad's lap, snuggled against his flannel shirt; my brother, Tom, too old to cuddle but sitting close, while we watched the lightning from the deck at our cabin; Dad teaching us not to be afraid, telling us that the universe is a friendly place.

Rivulets of molten gold sizzled through the darkness. From the bunk beds, I heard a chant, "One, one thousand, two . . .."

Thunder boomed, then grumbled away into the distance. "Wow, that was close." Currents of awe rippled in Travis' voice. I wondered why I hadn't heard Bear whining.

Squinting at the bed, I was able to make out two small shapes side by side in the lower bunk.

"Heather?" Jordan spoke quietly. "Want to sit on our bed?"

"I'd love to. But where's Bear?"

"He's with us." The dog snuggled between the two boys; each had an arm around him. "He was scared."

Travis said, "Did you get scared, Heather?"

"Not because of the storm. I had a bad dream."

"What about?" Jordan asked.

"A girl wearing red high heels. It seemed like she wanted to talk to me." There must have been a message in the dream. "But she was dead."

The boys were both quiet for about a heartbeat, then Travis said, "Mariella wore red high heels."

Jordan chimed in. "Yeah. Everybody says she just went off with Charlie again but, like, I don't think so.

She told us, 'no more Charlie,' and I believed her."

Lightning flashed, and suddenly, I smelled French fries as clearly as if a heaping plate were right in front of me. Then the pictures flooded back. The night I sneaked back to the cabin against the sheriff's advice, Mariella had brought my sandwich, with fries. I saw her marching across that wood deck at the Key of C Restaurant, wearing those red high heels.

My head spun. I felt dizzy and disoriented and afraid of what I might know. I gripped the edge of the bed. My mouth started to jabber. "I remember now. I met her. She had a new boyfriend, like you said. She told me his name was Ken Lagazo, and he had a red sports car, and he stood her up. It was the same night I got hurt."

"Oh, man." Jordy grabbed my arm and sucked in a loud breath. "That's the last day anybody saw her. What if you are the very last person she talked to, and you don't even know it?"

Travis said, "Jeannie says Charlie's insane when it comes to Mariella. What if he beat her up again and killed her by mistake? I bet he did, and he buried her in the woods somewhere far away from where he pushed her car down the hill. That's why they didn't find her."

We didn't count the seconds after the next flash. Instead, we huddled together and went over and over what we knew about Mariella. The thunder passed off to our right, toward town. Wind shook the branches of the old pear tree that hung over the deck, and the clouds opened up, releasing a torrent. Huge drops drummed on the metal roof and gurgled along the dusty gutters.

As we talked, Jake's words burned in my ears, "Tell me. Tell no one but me."

Too late for that.

When the storm passed on, I reminded them that we didn't know Mariella was dead and swore them to secrecy. Jordy climbed back into the top bunk, and I took Bear with me to my room. As I put my head on the pillow and pulled the blanket over me, I wanted to know the whole story. And I didn't. I wondered why I had been given my secure and caring family, while Mariella had to make her own way in the world. Life hadn't been fair to her. She had been left vulnerable to men like Charlie.

Every time my eyes closed and I started to drift off, the vision of Mariella, hanging upside down, her throat bloody and gaping open, yanked me back. I stared into the blackness. Was she dead, and if so, why? When I finally fell asleep, I dreamed that Bill Harlan stole my dad's boat and took it out fishing, then sneaked it back into our boathouse with an ice chest full of rotten fish heads on board.

When I woke up, I lay in bed and thought about Bill for a while. There was something creepy about his attention. He had never been anything more than polite before. Now he was downright solicitous. Could it be Mary was right, that he was looking to divorce Julie and replace her with someone else—like me? Ugh.

Mary was up before me. She and the boys were in the kitchen, playing poker at the yellow Formica and chrome table. Rain streaked the window, steadily setting up new pathways from top to bottom. The radio was on and it was ten o'clock—time for the Koffee Hour, the local call-in radio show.

The first caller's voice was deep and resonant. He sounded as if he should be announcing classical music and chatting about Beethoven. Instead, he asked if anyone knew anything about Mariella and where she might be. Our little group fell silent. He offered a reward to anyone who contacted him at the Chop Shop.

I glanced at Mary. "The Chop Shop?"

"They customize motorcycles," Travis said. "All the old biker guys hang out there."

"In Wenatchee," Jordy said. "I bet that was Charlie. Maybe he didn't kill her. Maybe he wants to go fight her new boyfriend, man, and get her back like he did before."

"Yeah," Travis said. "Or maybe she's hiding out so Charlie can't find her. Jeannie said Charlie would beat the you-know-what out of her."

"I guess I can believe that." Mary's mouth went into an unhappy, down-turned line. "But listen. Mariella's been on her own a long time. She'll turn up when she gets around to it."

I drew a long breath. If only I could agree. In my heart, I felt certain she was dead, that Charlie killed her, and now he was covering up.

Just before lunch, the sky cleared. Mary and the boys went off to visit friends. As soon as I was alone, I phoned Jake to tell him what I remembered about Mariella, but I had to leave a message. I waited impatiently for him to call me back. Whereas before, he had been hounding me to try to remember, now he didn't seem to be in a hurry to hear what I had to tell him, as if I wasn't all that important anymore.

I felt restless and prickly. I paced around the cabin, wishing I was back at the theater, painting sets, helping Janice sew costumes, and most of all, practicing for the lead role in *Taming*. Instead, I was merely marking time. My life was on hold. Until my liver healed and Dr. Mendosa okayed me to drive, and until Jake said I could leave, I was stuck.

Rumbling engines, throbbing slightly out of sync, jarred me out of my funk. I heard a roar from somewhere on the service road behind the cabins and hurried out onto the deck in time to see a parade of motorcycles round onto the lawn in front of the cabins. They headed toward the inn on the far side. Seventeen in total, riding two abreast, following a single leader. To a man, each rider was encased in denim and black leather studded with silver that gleamed in the sun.

Charlie! He had to be among them. But no. These were old guys, graying, wrinkled, paunchy. Most of them looked at least forty. Old guys playing out their fantasies. Not one of them matched my picture of Mariella's possessive boyfriend. They rode all the way across the lawn, past the inn, and disappeared. A moment later, I heard them coming back down the service road behind the cabins. Oh, man, this could not be good.

I rushed to the kitchen and grabbed my phone. As I dialed 911, I hurried back outside, begging the dispatcher to send Jake.

In the middle of the lawn, the leader raised a hand and signaled a stop. A long fringe swayed from his uplifted gauntlet. Riveted, I watched as he dismounted. Ceremoniously, he removed his gloves. Then he opened his silver-encrusted jacket, shrugged it off, and tossed it to the man behind him. Two by two, the others shut their rides down, then sat back, booted feet planted on either side of their shining, tricked-out bikes.

The leader strode toward me, long brown hair

curling and floating behind him in the soft breeze. At most, he was five-ten, and he looked sort of scrawny, all sinewy and wiry. But as he came closer, I saw what there was of him was muscle. He wore a tank top, tight, well-worn jeans, and a sleeveless leather vest. A diamond studded one ear, and a blue and red paisley tattoo covered one shoulder and curled up from under the tank top toward the diamond.

Warm, melodious tones flowed out of his mouth. "Good afternoon."

I recognized the voice from the Koffee Hour, the one Jordan thought was Charlie. I felt certain Jordan was right. I felt equally certain that this man had killed Mariella and had tried to kill me. My knees started to shake, and my mouth went completely dry. I searched for Bear's collar with my fingertips.

Chapter Twelve

"Tell me," he said, "where is the office?"

I couldn't move. I could only quiver like a jellyfish on the beach. "I'm—I'm—this is not the office."

"Whoa." He came up the stairs onto the deck. "You look as if you've seen an apparition." He put his hand under my elbow. "Perhaps you should sit down." His breath smelled like a whiskey sour, all liquor with a bit of lemon tossed in for grins and giggles.

I gripped Bear's collar and stepped away. My lips felt as stiff as old leather. I forced them into a sick half-smile. And reminded my quaking brain he didn't recognize me because he'd only seen my back. In the dark. As I ran away down the road.

"The office?" he said. "I need information."

I glared at him. "What did you do to Mariella?"

He scowled, moved toward me. "Where is she?"

"Not here."

"Not even Mariella can disappear into thin air. She's got to be somewhere." The music in his voice had been replaced with hard, flat, angry tones. "I want to know where. I've got rights. She's carrying my kid."

Jake eased his car up behind the motorcycles and got out. I pulled in a deep breath. "Rights? What rights? You have no rights. Even if she were here, she'd have no obligation to see you. Besides, I think you know damn well where she is."

"Oh, my God. Women." Charlie's lips curled in a sneer and he leaned toward me. "You're dingier than she is." A cloud of whiskey wafted over me.

The sheriff ambled up onto the deck. "Howdy. I've been waiting for you to show up." A full head taller, he towered over the tattooed biker.

"How's that?" The man paused for a moment. "Cop," he added in a contemptuous tone. "I've been gone a couple of days. Where's my girl?"

Jake didn't even blink. "I'm thinking you could help me figure that out." He stood with his feet apart, weight balanced. "And while we're at it, you could tell me what you know about a body left under a tree in an orchard last winter."

Holding onto Bear, I edged away.

With a snort, Charlie stuck his hands on his hips. "This is starting to stink, as usual when you're around." Turning toward his gang, he raised his voice. "Hey, lookee here. We got *the man* here. A smart one. Fuckin' grade A smart."

The bikers smirked and grinned at one another. A couple of them made an elaborate show of swinging their legs over their machines and taking off their jackets. They strolled toward the cabin. The rest settled back again, arms folded.

Jake turned his back on them. "I need to ask you some questions." His voice was even and unhurried. "How about riding to town with me?"

"Hey, guys, anybody smell a barnyard?"

Grunts and guffaws and oinks came from Charlie's buddies.

By then, Bear and I had backed away far enough to feel the cabin wall behind me. There was something reassuring about the rough wood under my fingertips. I watched, Jake on my left, Charlie on my right.

He looked Jake up and down. "My girl's disappeared, and I'm wanted for questioning. That right, O'Toole?" He made "O'Toole" sound like a dirty word.

"After I dry you out a bit."

"I'm the one with the questions." Charlie shifted forward, like a boxer, onto the balls of his feet. "People don't just disappear. Where the fuck is she?"

Jake fixed him with a cold, hard stare. "How about you tell me where you've been the last few days?"

The biker began dancing around, swinging his fists. "Fuck you, cop!" His shoulders and arms bulged with strength, and he had to be fifteen years younger than Jake. In spite of his size, he could be dangerous.

"Aw, come off it, man."

That made Charlie's eyes bulge out. "Shove it, pig. We got old business and we got new business." He danced in close and took a tentative jab at Jake.

I dialed 911 again and yelled, "For God's sake, get me Angel Orlando. I need him now."

Bear's neck hair bristled as he gave his warning growl, low and insistent. He broke away from me and began slowly circling the two men, watching, waiting.

Charlie lunged. Jake sidestepped, reached out an arm, grabbed the biker's wrist, pulled, and a second later, the guy was airborne, flipping head over heels.

The deck shook as he landed flat on his back. He rolled over and got halfway up, shaking his head as if to clear it. Then he was on his feet again, dancing half circles around the sheriff, who pivoted, turned slightly away, one arm up in defense, the other hand fisted.

111

The two guys who had climbed off their bikes started up the steps, one behind the other. I pointed. "Bear. Rip them up."

While Bear dashed across the deck, Charlie landed a punch on Jake's jaw, hard enough to snap his head back. A trickle of blood showed up at the corner of his mouth and the biker got in a couple more hard hits.

My dog sailed off the deck. Forepaws extended, he hit the first man at shoulder height, and they both went down like dominoes. Bear hovered over his victims, his growl thrumming over the air and mingling with their curses.

I shouted, "Hold, Bear."

Jake brought up a fist. The motorcyclist's head flew back. As it rebounded, the sheriff hit him again, and he staggered backward, arms flopping. Two more of the gang had stepped up onto the lawn, but kept their distance. The rest sat and watched.

"We can stop anytime you want." The sheriff sounded a little short of breath, and I started to worry.

With a roar, Charlie charged back. He swung upward into Jake's stomach, then got in a couple of blows to his head as he doubled over. I yanked the screen door open. An oar stood in the corner of the porch. I grabbed it. Jake smacked Charlie's head from side to side. The biker wrapped his arms around O'Toole's waist like a Sumo wrestler.

I swung the oar as hard as I could, aiming for Charlie's head. Instead, I got his butt. The motion caused pain to rip through my chest; I stumbled back against the cabin wall. The sheriff's hand chopped down on the back of the paisley-tattooed neck. The biker's knees buckled, and he crumpled into a heap, then flattened out on the deck, face down.

Wiping his hand across his bloody mouth, the sheriff took a couple of steps backward. Nobody moved. Absolute silence. As I looked around, I saw a little flock of nervous-looking mothers down the beach, well beyond the line of bikes, holding onto their kids.

Jake spoke between puffs of breath as he pulled out his ironed and folded white handkerchief. "You okay, Heather?"

I gasped in some air. "I'm glad I hit him. I feel much better." I wanted to cheer for the good guys. It was almost as good as when the UW Huskies scored a touchdown.

Jake nodded. "Whoo! Bit of a workout. Don't get much practice." He blotted his face. "Appreciate the help." He looked at the two men on the ground. "You could call Bear off now."

Stepping around Charlie's legs, I joined the sheriff by the stairs. "Bear, come."

As my dog obeyed, the two men lifted their heads and watched. They got to their feet and stood there, staring up at us, shamefaced. Bear and I stared back with contempt.

Mariella's boyfriend hadn't moved. I pointed at him. "Is he dead?" Not that I cared.

Sheriff O'Toole prodded Charlie's shoulder with the toe of his cowboy boot.

"Unnhh."

"I think that means no. Not dead."

I restrained myself from kicking the creep—once for Mariella and once for me—possibly only because Jake was there. The bastard deserved it. And a lot more. I clenched my fists. "I really, really, really want to kick him so hard he rolls right off the deck and down the stairs." With luck, he'd break his wretched neck.

Jake pressed his handkerchief against his lip. "I understand." He went to stand by Bear who still guarded the stairs. The two men had moved about halfway back to their bikes. Two others had joined them.

At that moment, a car skidded to a stop behind Jake's, lights flashing and dust rolling up behind it. With a grin, he looked at me. "You called the cavalry?"

"I called Angel," I said stiffly. As I spoke, the car door opened and a deputy—not Angel, to my disappointment—I was pretty sure Angel could handle any situation—stuck a pudgy leg out, then hoisted his bulk up, holding onto the top of the door.

Jake prodded Charlie again and was rewarded with a groan that ended in a string of words he probably had not learned at his mother's knee. "Good news, my friend. Another cop just showed up. Now you don't have to ride with me." He walked to the edge of the deck, put a hand on the rail and stared at the gang for a minute. I looked, too.

Matt, wearing baggy shorts and a big loose shirt, stood on the lawn beyond the row of motorcycles. His long blond hair was blowing around his expressionless face and sunglasses hid his eyes. Some teenagers stood near him, also watching. I wondered what Matt saw and what he knew; what secrets he was keeping. And how anyone could love a man who so readily shut you out of his inner thoughts.

"Hey, porker." One of the clustered bikers thrust up a forearm. "Ya got off easy. Charlie killed a man by accident once. With his bare hands."

Jake just stood there for a minute. Then he waved a hand. "Show's over." He made a little bow. "Thanks for coming, folks."

An engine began to throb, then another. Deep, muscular vibrations filled the air. Matt melted away toward Sam's house.

By then, the deputy had Charlie on his feet and handcuffed. With a beefy hand around his arm, he was marching him toward the stairs. His eyes, blazing with fury, met mine. "Bitch."

I didn't flinch. "And you're a son of a bitch."

Jake and I leaned on the railing and watched. Two by two, the gang paraded across the lawn. They picked up speed going past Sam's house, then roared up the driveway and thundered away toward town. Silence settled on the resort. Like a lawn ornament, Charlie's maroon and silver motorcycle stood where he'd left it. I looked for Matt. He was gone.

Beyond where he'd stood, out near the end of the dock, Travis, Jordan, and another boy brought an inflatable in and tied it up. They watched the bikers disappear and then walked slowly up to the cabin. Quietly. With none of their usual exuberant energy. They stopped at the bottom of the steps, and stood looking up at Jake and me, their faces solemn. Bear ran down to greet them. Jordy grabbed his collar the way I do when I'm scared.

My breath caught. Normally, they'd be jabbering about seeing that many huge, tricked-out motorcycles in one place. "What's wrong?" I asked. "Where's Mary?"

Jake joined me at the top of the stairs. "Usually I hear you guys coming miles away. What's got you pussy-footing around?"

"We hope we're not bothering you, Sheriff." Travis' voice sounded strained. "We have to show you something."

My stomach tightened into a knot.

Jake started down the steps. "You bet."

Jordy looked at me for a minute, then invited me to join them with a little motion of his hand. "In the boat."

We began a procession across the lawn toward the dock. Travis told us their friend's name was Christopher. He was taller than either Travis or Jordan and looked a little older. He had curly black hair, very dark eyes, and a friendly smile.

Travis said, "Aunt Mary's visiting his mom and we took Christopher's boat to go to the park to swim and fish and stuff."

"I take it something happened." Jake spoke slowly, his tone reassuring. "Something important."

"Yup." Travis nodded and rubbed the back of his arm across his forehead, wiping off sweat and making his dark hair stand up away from his brow. "We think it might be evidence, so we didn't touch it or anything."

It was Jordy who made me think something terrible was wrong. I'd never known him to be silent for more than fifteen seconds at a time, and so far, he'd barely spoken. I put my hand on his shoulder, half expecting him to react by clutching his throat and staggering about as if he were dying, as he normally did at signs of affection. Instead, he walked a little closer to me, sandwiching Bear between us.

We threaded our way through the sand-castle crowd to the dock. The boys' bare feet drummed lightly on the dry wood as Christopher led the way past the fuel pump, out toward the end. His boat turned out to be a fourteen-foot inflatable with an outboard motor, the kind many families keep so the kids can fish or scoot about the lake. He knelt on one knee to pull it closer to the dock, then refastened the lines to hold it there.

Bear, Jordy, and Travis climbed into the boat. They sat down, and Jordy watched as Travis unwound a blue and white beach towel, exposing a soggy red purse. Both boys looked up at Jake.

"It looks like Mariella's. We've seen her with it." Travis' words jolted through me. I sat down on the dock beside Christopher.

Jake got in the boat and sat beside Jordy. "Tell me what happened. Where and how did you find it?"

"We trolled up from Christopher's house on our way to the park." Travis gestured at their fishing rods, neatly stowed on one side of the boat. "When we were almost there, you know, just before the swimming area, Jordy thought he had a fish on, but it was this purse."

"Did you tell anyone else?"

Jordy shook his head. "No, sir. We came here. We were going to phone you."

We all watched as Jake opened the purse and extracted a worn coin pouch with a zipper on top. He opened it carefully, slid a thumb and finger inside, and pulled out a driver's license. After looking at it for a minute, he turned the purse over. It was a small shoulder bag, and the strap was broken at one end. "Looks like you're right. It's Mariella's." He gazed at the cousins.

Jordy said, "She could have dropped it in the lake by accident, Sheriff, couldn't she?" He pointed at the strap. "See, it's broken."

"Do you think that's how it came to be there, son?"

"No." He shook his head. "I just wish . . .."

"We all do, boys. We all do."

I mentally thanked Jake for the gentleness in his voice. Jordy was right. She wouldn't go anywhere without her purse. Mariella was not somewhere safe. Tears turned the boys into wavy, watery lines.

"It's not like when stuff like this happens on TV." Travis lowered his eyes. "Like, we know Mariella. She's nice."

"Yeah, she's sort of our friend." Jordy's voice trembled and it seemed to come from far away. My throat ached for these kids who shouldn't have to deal with this kind of stuff.

We were all quiet for a minute or two. Jake put the driver's license back in the coin purse, which he then tucked into the shoulder bag. He wrapped it back up in the towel and laid it on the seat beside him. "Would you show me right where you found it?"

They all nodded. While Travis and Jordan untied the lines, Christopher climbed in and sat in the stern. He started the motor.

My palms felt sweaty. "I'm coming along."

Easing into the boat, I sat down in the middle and reclaimed my dog. As we backed away from the dock, Jordy and Travis moved up to the bow. Jake joined Christopher at the back. We headed down-lake, toward town. In a few minutes, we passed the public boat launch with the dusty parking lot full of boat trailers, then the county park with picnic shelters and blue and red floats to mark the swimming area. Right after that, the hillside gets steep and the lake bottom falls away quickly, as it does at our cabin. Christopher slowed down. "We were right about here."

Travis surveyed the shoreline. "We were just about in line with the place where the skate board jump is."

Christopher put the engine in neutral and we coasted to a stop.

Travis pointed at a sturdy wooden structure angling from the edge of the road, which was five or six feet higher than the lake, out over the rocks. "That's where the high school guys zoom down the hill on their boards and fly off into the water." I wondered if their parents knew. It looked like a great place to break a few arms and legs.

Jake said, "Once in a while, when it's icy, a car will skid into the lake here. I want to look around on shore." Rough, brown, two-man rocks lined the edge of the lake, debris from blasting the hill away, pushed into the water to make a flat spot for the road. Apart from a few scrubby bushes, nothing grew there. I had never noticed before, but as close as it was to the county park, it felt bleak and remote. As competent as an adult, Christopher sidled the boat up to shore. Travis and Jordan braced their hands on the rocks to keep the boat from bashing against them. Jake stretched out a long leg and eased up onto solid ground.

As the boat rebounded, Travis picked up an oar and shoved us out a little way. The waves rocked us gently. We all leaned over the side and looked down, but saw nothing except our own wavering reflections.

Jordy said, "If it was icy and a car slid in, it would be close to shore. We'd be able to see it. But her purse was way out there." He pointed. "Besides, it's not even winter."

Chapter Thirteen

In Mary's back bedroom, darkness choked out all light. The summer night felt like velvet, soft and thick and warm. I tried to find a comfortable position in the narrow bed by resting my arm on a pillow so it didn't press against my ribs. That didn't work. I lay on my back but that made my neck ache. I plumped the pillow and turned it over, then over again. Too cool, I pulled the sheet up. A few minutes later, it was too hot. I pushed it down to my feet.

Every time my eyes closed, they popped open from the gnawing questions. Where was Mariella? Had she drowned? Had she lost her purse in some fluky way? Did Charlie or one of his thugs discard her purse in that spot, thinking it might never be found, or if it was found, that it would draw attention away from where she really was?

People say death by drowning is pleasant, that after a brief struggle, a kind of peace comes over you, but I found that hard to believe. In my mind, I saw Mariella, terrified and disoriented, holding her breath as long as she could and then gasping, pulling water into her lungs and choking. That had to be excruciating.

Jordy preferred to think that Charlie beat her up, that maybe he had killed her unintentionally. The word "accidentally" didn't work for me, as in, "oh, gee, I accidentally killed Mariella", even though it might make Jordy feel better. What is beating someone if not a desire to silence them? It's a very short step from beating to killing.

This disorderly hodgepodge of thoughts swirled through my head. It was like being trapped in a traffic circle, endlessly circling, trying to find a way to a safer, saner place while horns blared and cars charged in and out on all sides.

Jake said he didn't have a reason to hold Charlie. He'd let him go, in spite of my telling him I was certain Charlie had tried to kill me, too. So, there wasn't any evidence. That didn't mean he didn't do it, and it didn't mean he wouldn't try again. I shivered. On a night as black as that one, Charlie could be anywhere. I turned on the reading light Mary had clamped to the headboard for me and pointed it at the window.

Every night before going to bed, I checked the lock, even though she said the window frame had so many coats of paint holding it shut it would take a stick of dynamite to get it open. I eased out of bed to check it again. I slid my hand behind the blind and ran my fingers along the frame until I felt the cool metal lock, shaped like the letter C, firmly clasped. Imagining Charlie watching, seeing the light, seeing my arm, I jerked my hand back. I was covered with goose bumps.

Jake said someone was keeping an eye on me, but if that was true, I had no idea who it was. I had never seen him. I wanted Angel Orlando sitting in the corner of my room the way he did in the hospital, or better yet, we'd all be safer if he would sit in the porch, to make sure no one broke the flimsy hook that held the squeaky screen door shut against the world.

On tiptoes, I walked past Mary's room and out to

the porch. The only thing that separated us from the outside world was that little hook. I stared at it for a minute, then snapped my fingers. Bear's nails scraped across the old wood floor. His white blaze was faintly visible in the ambient light. "Come, Bear."

He liked sleeping in the porch with the boys. It was about ten degrees cooler out there, but he followed me back to the bedroom, and when I straightened my sheets and climbed back into bed, he settled down on the rug beside me. Reaching for furry comfort, I put my hand over the side of the bed. "Well, we outsmarted him once, didn't we, Bear?" And his accomplice, the other man in the boat, undoubtedly one of his gang.

As the first light of dawn reached through the blinds over the window and touched the curtain, I closed my eyes.

****

"Hea-eather!" The screen door banged shut. "Hea-eather!" From a deep sleep, I came suddenly to full awareness. Bright sunlight filled my room.

"In here, guys." I rolled to my side and pushed straight up to my feet. The sound of bare feet running on wood floors. Then the boys burst through the doorway and stopped short.

"Heather, they found . . ." Travis put a hand over his mouth. "Sorry we woke you up."

"Geez, Heather, you missed a major event already." Jordan's eyes were wide and round and a shock of red hair stood up away from his forehead.

"Mariella. They found her," Travis said. "In a car."

Jordy elbowed Travis in the ribs. "*I'm* talking. She's right where we showed the sheriff yesterday. He's getting a tow truck. We're going to watch."

I felt the blood drain from my face. Suddenly dizzy, I had to sit on the bed.

"You okay?" Jordy asked.

"How?" I heard myself mumble, "When?"

"Matt's a scuba diver," Travis said.

"We showed him where to look," Jordan said. "Mom took us in the boat."

Mary appeared in the doorway. "You two scram. Go find yourselves some orange juice." She turned to watch as they ran down the hall, then she closed the door and leaned against it. "This is so awful. The boys have decided it was an accident. I'd like to think so, but something tells me it wasn't." Tears filled her eyes and spilled onto her cheeks.

Numb to the core, I couldn't speak. In the pit of my stomach, I knew she was right.

Sniffing, Mary wiped away tears with her fingertips. "I'm not sure they should watch, but there's no way to shield them from the fact that she's dead, and they want to see how they get the car out." She went to the dresser, pulled up a tissue, and blew her nose. "We won't get close, and if it looks bad, we'll leave."

I got to my feet and willed my knees not to buckle. "It wasn't an accident."

Mary shook her head. "I really thought she'd just gone off somewhere."

Drained of hope, neither of us had anything more to say. "I wish you'd been right."

The aroma of coffee filled the kitchen by the time I got there. Mary poured two cups, and we all headed for her runabout. I wondered if we were being ghoulish, but at the same time, I wanted to be there. Mariella had faced her death all alone. I didn't want her to be alone when they brought her back to the surface. It seemed like the right thing to do. If even a tiny part of her spirit lingered, she would know she had friends who cared. I twisted my fingers into the hair on Bear's neck, and although I didn't truly believe, I prayed that God would have mercy on her soul.

Sam Fitzpatrick's white cabin cruiser waited, idling, a short distance off the dock. I remembered how he patrolled the mouth of our cove the day of the murder. Whereas before, pieces of that day had lurked in the back of my mind like faded, old, sepia-toned photographs with dry, curling edges, now that entire terrible time was as crisp and clear as if it had never gone missing. As Mary headed out, Sam lifted a hand in greeting, then eased his throttle open and came along beside us, like a sheep dog herding sheep. I remembered how Matt, introduced that day as Dave, had stayed out of sight in the cabin of the boat, hidden behind curtained windows, until it was time to get in the water. The curtains were closed now, as opaque as Matt himself, and I wondered if he was hiding again.

When we got there, Mary cut the motor. Sam did the same and drifted off to our port side, between us and the body of the lake. For a moment everything was still, and then, on shore, a huge tow truck, glimmering with bright red paint, backed to the edge, right beside the skate board jump. Jabbered out, Jordy and Travis watched in silence. Jake took a couple of chocks off the truck and kicked them under the rear wheels. The driver fed out a thick cable with a mammoth hook at the end. Matt, wearing a black dive suit, stood on the rocks at the edge of the water. He hoisted a scuba tank onto his back, grabbed the hook, and tumbled into the water.

"Matt has to be FBI," Mary said. "Think about it. The first night, when he came for dinner, I asked what he did. He said he has a big desk in a big building with hundreds of other ants who crawl in and out. Then he changed the subject."

Her hazel eyes were alert and bright beneath the auburn bangs and broad-brimmed sun hat. "It all fits. My father had a couple of buddies in the Bureau. I used to try to get them to tell me about their work, and I'd be thinking they had, but the next day, I'd remember what they said and realize it was a lot of hot air. They're trained to do that. They divert you the way a magician diverts your attention from one hand by doing something tricky with the other hand." She stuck the tip of a finger in her mouth and chewed at the nail. "Yup. Matt's good at it. He's got to be FBI."

I said, "I don't think the feds investigate murders."

"Precisely." Eyebrows raised, she tilted her head toward the boys, and spoke very quietly. "It could be that Jake asked for help, but I'm beginning to wonder if what we're seeing is something more sinister." She put a finger to her lips, but the boys were not listening.

Their eyes were glued on Matt. As he snorkeled away from shore, the driver played out the cable from the back of the truck. He tucked and for a second, his big black fins hovered in the air. Then they slid down into the water, leaving only a ripple. On shore, Jake stalked back and forth in the sunshine, hands on his hips, as if he hadn't noticed how still and hot it was.

Out in the boat, with no breeze to speak of and the sun glaring off the surface of the water, it was brutal. Jordy rolled his eyes back until only the whites showed. "Mom, I'm dying of heatstroke right now."

"If you put on a life vest, you may jump in the lake," she offered.

"Okay." Within a minute the boys were bobbing in the lake.

"Stay right here." Mary sounded stern. "I don't want you anywhere near that cable."

I considered joining them, but settled for dipping my hand in the water and rubbing it over my face.

As Travis and Jordan paddled around the boat, I said, "Maybe Charlie is trafficking drugs, and Mariella knew too much, and he was afraid she'd talk. If that's the case, Matt could be working for the DEA."

"You could be right." Mary squinted, keeping an eye on the tow truck. "Maybe she threatened to blow the whistle on Charlie if he didn't quit dealing."

We were both silent for a couple of minutes, then Mary said, "I know this doesn't make sense, but for some weird reason, I'd feel better if it wasn't just Charlie's jealous temper that killed Mariella."

"That's weird all right. But I get it."

Matt's black hood broke the surface and he swam to shore. A minute later, a grinding, whining noise told us that the tow truck had begun to roll up the cable. Mary leaned over the side. "I'd like you two to get back in here, please."

"Okay." Scrambling to be first, pushing at each other, they climbed over the transom. They wrapped themselves in beach towels and popped open juice cans.

The rear end of a red car showed up, bumping slowly toward the tow truck. I held my breath as the cable continued to pull. The vehicle emerged inch by inch. It lurched backward over the rocks.

"An Italian sports car," Travis crooned.

Mariella's words reverberated in my mind. "I have dibs, don't forget." Good God! If only she had known.

The windshield stared back at us. The driver's door hung open and the seat was empty. On the other side, a bloated, once-slender arm and hand dangled from the window.

Chapter Fourteen

We had to face the fact that our little vacation
community was not the same safe, idyllic place it had
always been. We couldn't hope that Mariella appear out
of the blue at Sam's some morning, ready to go to
work. Nor would she show up to wait tables at the Key
of C Restaurant in town. And there was nothing we
could do about it.

Some people are sweet and nice all the time, no
matter what happens. As it turns out, I'm not one of
them. I had to see the doctor that afternoon but needed
Jake's permission to leave the resort. I needed Mary to
drive me with Angel or one of the other deputies
following. It made me crazy that I couldn't just get in
my car and go, but there was nothing I could do about
that, either. I wanted to punch someone in the nose.

When Angel Orlando showed up, ready to follow
us to town, Mary called Travis and Jordan to get in the
car. In the back seat, the boys argued about which of
them was smarter, Jordy more loudly than Travis. Mary
ignored them.

I gritted my teeth and tried to think of something
positive, but after a couple of minutes gave up on that.
Instead, I whined, "Do we have to listen to Jordan
bellowing from the back seat?"

She snapped back, "It's my car."

We were all feeling the strain of Mariella's death.

No one was immune. And my self-pity wasn't going to help. As we approached the county park, I addressed my faux pas. "I'm sorry I said Jordy was a pain."

Mary sighed. "It's okay. He *is* a pest sometimes." She offered a tight little smile. "After all, they *are* men in training."

We both sighed. Then Mary glanced at her son in the mirror. "Jordan, Travis, that's quite enough."

Instantly, they went silent, as if they were grateful to stop, as if, by arguing, they had been begging for an adult to take charge.

In the air-conditioned comfort of Mary's car, we glided past the park. When we came to the skate board jump, yellow crime scene tape stretched all the way around it and halfway across the road. Jake, who was starting to take the tape down, put up a hand, signaling Mary to stop. She did, and while we waited, a large, windowless, white van lumbered up onto the road in front of us. It headed up the hill toward town.

We all stared. There was no sign of the red car or the big red tow truck. If we hadn't been there, I wouldn't have believed that Mariella had been brought back to the surface only a few hours before. I wondered if she was in the van ahead of us, on her way to autopsy, to be cut open. I shuddered.

Jordy said, "Okay, look how steep the hill is right here. Say they're coming from town and he's driving fast. That car would go like a rocket. Then a deer jumps out on the road. The guy swerves and loses control, and they go shooting off into the lake."

I wished I thought it had happened like that. But I was pretty sure that Mariella's new boyfriend, Ken Lagazo, was the man I'd seen murdered, that he was at the bottom of my cove, and that it had been Charlie who drove Ken's car into the lake—intentionally. All he had to do was pick Mariella up in it and make sure she drowned while he escaped. He had plenty of muscles. He would have been able get out once it was in the water. And if he drugged her first, she wouldn't have struggled with him. It would have been easy.

Jordy was still talking ten minutes later when we pulled into the parking lot at the doctor's office. "Maybe there wasn't a deer. Maybe he was groping her up and lost control."

Mary's head swiveled around. "*Groping her up*? I beg your pardon, young man."

Jordan leaned forward to answer his mom, arms crossed on his chest. No hidden agenda with this kid. If he thought something should be said, he said it. There was something reassuring about that. I slid out of the car, and Angel escorted me into the clinic.

By the time Dr. Alicia Mendosa entered the exam room, my ribs throbbed with each breath and the ache in my back had turned hard and ugly.

In one hand, she held a slip of paper, which she looked at, more than once, and frowned. "It appears your liver's not doing so well."

I'd had blood drawn the day before. No doubt she was looking at the results.

From my perch on the exam table, I frowned back. "Why don't you prescribe something to fix it?" To my own ears, I sounded like a snotty thirteen-year-old. I couldn't imagine what she thought—though in her job she must be used to cranky patients.

She pulled herself up her full five feet four inches. "I cannot *fix* your liver." Her cheeks flushed dark red.

She tossed back her abundant black hair and fastened her dark brown eyes on mine. "Your lab reports are worse than they were when you left the hospital. That tells me you have not done such a hot job of following my orders. You must rest, drink plenty of water. Rest. Eat small balanced meals. *And rest.*"

"Fine. Fine. I'll do that. But I'll do it in Seattle." I slid off the table and flipped that ridiculous white cotton rectangle off over my head, then marched to the chair for my T-shirt. I'd call Grandma Garnet. She'd send a car, and I'd be home tomorrow.

Dr. Mendosa took a breath, then let it out in a sigh that went on forever. I realized she had been working hard all day, all week in fact, on her feet in that stuffy building, patching up some little kid who had been screaming while I waited, and who knew what else.

"This must be difficult for you," she said with more patience than I currently displayed. "But please, don't risk hurting yourself." Her tone was even and quiet. "I shouldn't have snapped at you. Most sincerely, I apologize."

I turned around, picked up the silly white cover, put it back on, and climbed back onto the exam table.

"Now, let me look at you." She peered at my eyes. "Just a tiny bit yellow." She had me lie down, thumped gently on my abdomen, and nodded when I winced. "Liver damage is tough. And it's serious. I really want to help you, but mostly it's up to you to follow your treatment plan."

When she had done all the usual doctor tasks, I promised to come to see her in three more days, and I promised to get more rest. I should have thanked her, and I wanted to, but I didn't. I felt as if she'd set me

131

back at least a week. It wasn't her fault. It was mine. But still. I had to stop doing the only thing that made me feel that I was getting stronger every day—walking laps on the service road behind the cabins at Sam's.

Soon after we got back to Mary's cabin, Jake came over to debrief. We all gathered at the table in the screened porch. He swore us to silence about what we had seen and what we knew—or thought we knew. He looked each of the boys in the eye and they promised.

"I have more," he said, "for Heather's ears only. You can sit in, Mary. It's time you heard."

She shooed the kids off, to Jordy's disgust. Jake, Mary, and I huddled together. He leaned across the table toward us and spoke quietly. "Mariella died of blows to her head, prior to immersion in the water."

The news hit me with a physical force, as if Jake had slapped me. I felt sick.

Just then, Jordy stomped up the stairs, dripping blood from a large, dirty scrape on his arm. "I jumped off the tree swing and landed wrong."

While Mary went inside to clean up the wound, Jake continued, "Blows—plural. Mariella sustained multiple blows to her head."

"Just like the water-skier." My pulse pounded at my temples. "Ever since I woke up this morning, I've remembered it all. That's what they did to him."

His brows went clear to his hairline. "Please start at the beginning and tell me exactly what you remember. Leave nothing out. I need to be absolutely certain you recall everything that happened that day."

When I finished, he said, "Sounds to me like you are spot on. I'll write up your report. Tomorrow you can read it over, then sign it."

I held my head in one palm. "The worst part is that one of them was laughing while they clubbed him."

Jake looked grim. "Some people actually enjoy the act of killing. They get a thrill out of having ultimate control of another person. Often, they make a game of it to draw things out, knowing they can take their victim's life at any moment, and there's nothing he or she can do about it."

"Charlie." A rush of hatred boiled up from the center of my gut, making my heart pound. "Mariella didn't deserve that. I wish I *had* kicked him yesterday."

"It's true that Charlie has a hair-trigger temper. But he's innocent until proven guilty, and we don't have anything on him. And don't forget, there were two men in the boat." Jake pressed his lips together, drew his shaggy brows down over his deep brown eyes, and gazed at me. "I'm reminding you of this so you won't let down your guard. Don't trust anyone."

Mary and Jordan rejoined us at that point, and we admired his bandaged arm. Then Jake went off to tell Sam how Mariella died, and Jordan went back to the tree swing.

Mary sounded uncharacteristically gloomy. "If Jordy hadn't hooked her purse, Mariella might never have been found."

"I can't believe no one saw anything," I said.

"Someone may well have seen something. Lots of killers get away because people refuse to get involved. Dad drummed this into me practically every day—the law is everyone's responsibility. We can't just leave everything to the cops."

We speculated some more, until I felt totally wrung out, empty. I'm ashamed to say that a tiny, unworthy part of me rejoiced. Because I was still alive. Because someone else—Mariella—not me—was dead. I didn't want to admit it, even to myself. "I need to think about something else for a while. We need to take a break."

Mary stood up and headed for the kitchen. "I agree. I'm ready for a glass of wine. I'm sorry you can't have some, too, but I'll bring you some lemonade. Fortunately, it's movie night. We can put this out of our minds for a while."

I hoped she was right.

Chapter Fifteen

Sam Fitzpatrick loved old movies. According to Mary, he had a climate-controlled room in his basement where he stored his collection in big round metal canisters, and no one else was allowed to touch them. Every Friday night all summer long, he picked one out and set up a large screen on the patio and an old-fashioned home projector on his dining room table. He opened the window and pointed the lens across the patio at the big screen. It was a Lake Sterling tradition.

Dad always used to bring us. People would ramble from the cabins toward the patio. Others drove in from the neighborhood or walked over from the campground next door. They set up chairs and settled themselves amongst their soft drinks, sweaters, and blankets for the little ones. Sam always made bushels of popcorn and put it in an old washtub, and there was a lunch-sack full for everyone. He never charged a cent and I think he had more fun than anyone else, telling corny jokes and catching up on local gossip.

As the evening shadows stretched long across the lawn in front of the cabin, we ate left-over lasagna and then went inside to get ready. Desperate to cut the gloom, I tied a red and white kerchief around Bear's neck. Then I stood in the screened porch waiting for Mary to walk over to Sam's.

In total incongruity with the rest of the day, the

flower shop in town had delivered a bouquet of stargazer lilies just before Jake showed up to tell us how Mariella died. Their fragrance filled the porch, spread throughout the cabin, and spilled through the screens into the cooling air outside. I picked up the card and read it again: "You will never be able to imagine how much we miss you. Get back here now." I heard Janice's voice behind the words. It came from all the volunteers at Viva! and—surprise—Alex.

I lingered for a long minute over his name, picturing his winter-sky eyes and the smile that started with one corner of his mouth. My heart didn't flip and flop the way it used to and it no longer felt like it would break. Even when I tried to dredge them up, the familiar pangs of rejection felt dull and distant.

Travis and Jordan, their hair wet from the shower and smelling of shampoo, ejected themselves from the living room. As usual, Jordy was impatient to get started. "We took the chairs over already. Come on. It's getting dark."

Mary tossed a sweatshirt at him. "Here. We're right behind you. Travis, you've got yours, right?"

"It's already over there." He raced his cousin across the deck to the stairs and jumped from the middle of the flight down to the grass.

Mary rolled her eyes at the two. "Travis, your mom will skin me if you sprain your ankle."

"I won't." His voice, bright and optimistic, carried clearly in the quiet evening and echoed back off the hill behind the cabin. Crossing her fingers, Mary fell into step beside me.

That afternoon, when Jake came to talk, he had taken Bogey from the police impound yard, driven it out to Sam's, and parked it beside Mary's cabin. It felt great to have my car back, smashed in headlights, hood, bumper, and all. As we sauntered toward the movie, I gazed at it. The damage wasn't as bad as I had expected, but next to Mary's shiny new sedan, it looked dusty and worn, unloved. Only Alicia Mendosa's stern words about exertion ruining my liver for the rest of my life kept me from grabbing a bucket of warm, sudsy water and cleaning it up. Lord knows, you only get one liver each time around.

Out of the corner of my eye, I saw Bill Harlan pull in to the dock. Seeing his boat jolted me back to the day of the murder, when I'd taken Dad's identical speedboat out to search for the water-skier. Having my memory back wasn't all that great sometimes. I squelched the picture in my mind and tuned in again to Mary, who had continued talking. She said, "I'm going to chat with Sam and Penny about putting on a memorial service for Mariella."

It was the only thing I'd heard all day that made me feel better. "I'd like to help."

"Jake doesn't seem to think she has any family, at least not any who'd care."

We stepped onto the concrete patio beside Sam's house and the impromptu theater. The place looked just as it did every summer. Wooden half-barrels that served as planters stood here and there, overflowing with bright red geraniums and white daisies. Half a dozen round, wrought iron tables and their umbrellas had been moved out onto the grass to make room for rows of chairs, and about twenty-five people milled around. They moved to better spots, then back to the first places, got soft drinks from the vending machine beside the inn, and called to their kids to sit down.

Mary waggled her fingers at Penny, Sam's wife, who stood by the washtub full of popcorn, helping Jordan and Travis fill brown paper lunch sacks. Her slim figure, tousled pixie haircut, and enormous, expressive eyes always reminded me of Audrey Hepburn. As we approached, Penny sent me an appraising glance, then pressed her lips together and shook her head a little. Turning back to the boys, she scooped popcorn into the sack Jordy held open. When it was overflowing, he handed it to me.

It had been a long time since a freckle-faced date had smiled so innocently over the top of a bag of popcorn. "It's got real butter on it," he said. It was so sweet, I nearly cried.

Jake O'Toole raised the big white screen and maneuvered it back and forth while Sam focused the projector and yelled directions from the dining room. When they had it lined it up so the picture was clear and centered, Sam turned the projector off.

Bill Harlan bent over the washtub and filled a sack, then eased over my way. He tapped a finger against his temple. Lines of tension marked his forehead, but he looked concerned, and his smile seemed friendly. "Your memory? How's that doing?"

Jake scooped up a handful of popcorn and came to stand beside Bill, munching and staring at me. Solemn. The man's conception of supervision was getting on my nerves.

I sucked in a breath and lied, just as Jake expected. "The doctor says the days around my accident are probably gone forever." I grinned to show that everything was marvelous. "That's okay with me."

Bill smirked. "Bet you're a little stir crazy by now. Come on up to my place. Julie's still away, but I really can cook. How about dinner tomorrow?"

"Thanks," I cooed. "I'll let you know."

There! That would give old Jake a nightmare or two. Sliding my hand into the pocket of my shorts, I curled my fingers around the ignition key for poor, crumpled Bogey. The key to independence. Even if Jake would have a cow.

"Looks like Sam's about ready," Jake said. "Heather?" He indicated a chair, then, still glaring, sat beside me.

Bill winked and sat on my other side.

So what did the good sheriff think I'd do? Jump Bill's bones while Julie was away?

I love old movies and *The African Queen* is my all-time favorite. As soon as Sam started the projector, the title flashed up on the screen. The sound track began. It lifted me up and teleported me back in time to the early days of World War I, and from Lake Sterling to German East Africa. By the time Humphrey Bogart made his stomach-rumbling appearance at Katherine Hepburn's proper tea table, they had become Charlie Allnut, the disheveled riverboat captain, and Rose Sayer, the prim spinster missionary.

Charlie and Rosie, who in spite of initial prejudice and dislike, join forces to strike a blow for England by sinking a German gunboat. Beset by stinging insects and death-defying rapids, then trapped in reeds and half-eaten by leeches, doomed to failure, they fall in love. When their boat sinks from under them, they are rescued by the German gunboat they tried to torpedo and the captain sentences them to hang.

As always, I had to wipe away tears when Charlie asked the captain to marry them first. Obviously, their romance had been planned from the beginning of time, destined. I wanted that. Someday, when I wasn't even expecting it, true love would come. Rosie and Charlie. Heather and . . ..

"THE END".

Way too soon, those words crashed rudely across the screen. Even though the breeze was making goose bumps on my bare legs, I wasn't ready to be jerked back to reality. Around me, everyone stood and stretched, laughing and talking.

Mary said, "Penny invited us for ice cream. Let's go on in."

I stepped into a huge country kitchen. Glossy yellow cupboards ran all the way up to the high ceiling. They made the room look as if it were bathed in spring sunshine, and set off the handsome black granite counter tops. A round oak table stood at the far side, covered with a checkered blue cloth.

Penny looked over her shoulder as she opened the refrigerator. "I'm glad you can join us." She pulled out a pitcher of milk and headed for the table, stopping on the way to grab an ice cream scoop out of a drawer. No wonder she was such a skinny little thing. She was always going ninety miles an hour.

Matt sauntered in and headed straight for the ice cream freezer that sat in the sink, turning in its bucket of ice. "Looks like it's slowing." He stuck a pencil in the drain hole and wiggled it back and forth. When he removed the pencil, a stream of water gushed out.

Penny looked at it over his shoulder. "D'you think it's done, Matt?"

"Almost." He turned toward me. "Heather." He peered at my face, then lifted my chin with his fingertips. "Your bruises are starting to fade."

An electric tingle followed in the wake of his touch. I forgot I was mad at him. I forgot I'd sworn off men. I wanted more touch, more tingle, more, more, more, and very soon—soon and often. Rosie and Charlie. Heather and . . . Matt?

I stood there for a second with my mouth open. Then, totally muddled, I started toward the table. Geez, get a grip. I turned back to face him. "Look, I have some questions to ask you."

"Sure." He turned back to the sink. Like, sure, he really wanted to talk to me.

Travis and Jordan burst in and swarmed right up beside him, saving him. "Oh, man, home-made." Jordy rubbed his stomach.

Everybody circled the table while Matt lifted the shiny metal cylinder out of the bucket of ice, wrapped a towel around it, and carried it over. He scooped fresh strawberry ice cream into frosty bowls and Penny handed them around. It was the kind of stuff that made me wonder why I bothered to eat anything but dessert.

Matt was watching me from across the table, a little smile on his face. When I looked at him, he ducked his head.

The kitchen filled with happy sounds, but Jake hunched over his bowl, methodically spooning up his ice cream. He was holding something back. What?

A picture of Mariella's arm hanging out of the window of the red car hit me. A lump of concrete landed in my stomach.

Jake stood. "Penny, thank you. But now I have to

talk with the fella who made the ice cream."

"Okay." Penny waved a hand at Jake. "Shoo. The rest of us are going to play sevens."

I watched Jake, then Matt, vanish through the door into the hallway. I tried to concentrate on the game, but couldn't. Pushing my chair back, I asked, "Penny, where's your bathroom?"

"Go up one flight." She pointed at the door the men had gone through. "We'll deal you in again when you get back."

I knelt beside Bear. "Let me fix your necktie." My heart beat faster as I unfastened my locket with the tracer in it. I untied his kerchief, rolled the locket up in it, then put it back around his neck and got to my feet.

In the hall, soft light from a pair of sconces led me to the stairway. I started up the creaky wood treads, resting my hand on the wide, smooth banister. The second floor was dim and quiet. No light escaped under closed doors. I heard nothing.

I inched up, stopping and holding my breath every time a board creaked. At the top, the ceiling sloped down from the peak in the middle, and a hallway ran the length of the floor, with doors on each side. Close by, two doors stood open, one across from the other, allowing the cool night breeze to blow through. A pale greenish light came from the room on the right, and male voices.

I crouched in the shadow of the thick newel post. So far, it had been way too easy. Just as I decided to sneak closer, Jake's voice rose to a near shout. "I can't buy it. That slime ball's walking around free. In my county. He's dangerous. I'm going to arrest the jerk. Tonight. Before Heather gets hurt again."

My heart lurched at the implications in his words.

"If you arrest him now, you'll blow the whole operation," a distinct Midwest accented voice said. I hadn't heard it before. "Those guys have him on a very short leash. By this time tomorrow, they'd know you picked him up. And you know what would happen as well as I do. They'd go to the ground for a few weeks, and then they'd set up shop somewhere else. All you'd be doing is kicking the can down the road."

"We have to wait," Matt cautioned. "It won't be long. Devine isn't the kind to leave a bungled attempt on his record. His reputation is on the line. He'll be back soon. And then we'll get all of them. In the meantime, as long as everyone thinks Heather still has amnesia, she's safe."

"One hundred percent guaranteed? Are you telling me the mighty FBI won't botch it up?" Jake bit his words off and spat them out. "So I'm just a back-country sheriff. You should have told me months ago when I found the guy in the orchard. I could have been on the watch. For damn sure I would have protected Heather better and maybe saved Mariella."

"That's all water under the bridge." The Midwest voice sounded loud and harsh. "We have our eyes on Heather every second. I tell you, no one will get to her."

"Baloney!" Jake bellowed. "A million things could go wrong."

"Look at these goddamn monitors." It was the third man again. "We know what's in her cereal bowl, for Chrissake. We hear every fart. If anyone gets anywhere close, we'll know. We'll be there."

Blood rushed in my ears. Still crouching, I inched forward. If Jake was taking orders from this guy, I had to find out who he was.

I heard Jake's cowboy boots stomping back and forth. "Let me tell you something." His voice vibrated with anger. "Murder in Sterling County is my responsibility. The safety of the people in Sterling County is my responsibility. I have a known perp. With the right kind of pressure, he might do the job for Devine. He's already tried."

There was a loud hollow clunk, like maybe he'd kicked a metal waste basket.

I flattened myself to the wall and moved toward the open door just as Matt said, "It was a half-hearted attempt, and Orlando foiled it."

My head started to spin. Half-hearted attempt at what? Against whom?

"I don't care." Jake wasn't buying it. "It's a mighty big risk and you know it."

The Midwest accent butted in. "Look—he hasn't got the guts. Devine will be back."

"Fuck you both," Jake bellowed. "Fuck your grand plan to hang Heather out for bait. You don't have a clue what a sicko gun-for-hire devil like Devine will do. He's smart. He's slick. He's a master of deception, and he moves around the globe like a phantom."

"I have some other concerns, Jake," Matt said. "All you've got is pieces of the boat—*a* boat. It's not enough evidence. Could be anybody's boat."

My spine jerked straight. Jake had found the boat?

Matt continued. "You're relying on an eye witness who can't identify anyone. And she's had amnesia. No prosecutor will take that on. Even if he did, the defense would tear her testimony apart." His tone softened. "You know that—knew it before I was born, no doubt."

Jake's "Shit!" reverberated around the attic. "Dammit."

I peeked into the room. A couple of times, late in the evening, I'd seen the man with the Midwest accent, smoking down by the lake. He was short and round and bald, with a small, pinched mouth. My heart sank. Travis and Jordan had talked about him. They called him Smiley because he never smiled or spoke to anyone. This out-of-shape lump of lard was responsible for keeping me safe? Seriously? For a moment, all I could do was stare at him.

"Listen," Matt said, "we have a chance to find the body in Heather's cove. Then you'd have a solid case."

Sarcasm dripped from Jake's voice. "Don't tell me the FBI's had a change of heart."

"No, but I have a friend at UW who is working on a PhD in physics, building a sub that runs on alternative power sources."

I could hardly believe what I was hearing. I was bait, and now it was amateur hour. My blood started to boil. I stalked into the room. "Oh, great—yay for me!" I shouted. "Saved by a sardine can that runs on peanut butter."

"Actually, it's driven by alternate compression and expansion of gases as they heat up and cool off." Matt stopped. His mouth hung open for a few beats. "What are you doing here?"

The darkest parts of me, those that I kept stuffed way down inside, surged to the surface. My face burned with indignation. I was Kate the Shrew at her best.

"How dare you! You and your pretty little Live Like King Tut fable. You kiss me and tell me you liked it. You say you are my biggest fan. You pretend to bare your soul. You think I can't figure out what's going on? All you want is for me to believe that you're a good guy, so you can leave me hanging out for a pack of wolves. So I can end up as dead as Mariella. Well, damn you all to hell!"

Slick as spit, Matt reached out and took my hands. "It's not like that."

I wrenched away. "Keep away from me, you—you Judas!"

Jake said, "Heather, listen. I spoke out of turn. Matt's right. We must wait. We will keep you safe. I promise."

"How safe am I if I can get up here without you knowing? I trusted you."

Jake pursed his lips, nodded.

"You could have trusted me," I yelled. "You could have told me."

"Point taken. Now let's see your tracer."

The guy with the Midwest accent broke in. "Uh, guys, the tracer appears to be malfunctioning. Hear this?" He pointed at a speaker.

I knew that sound. It was the tracker clinking against Bear's bowl while he licked the remnants of ice cream from it, determined to get every atom of goodness. I was supposed to depend on this imbecile? "Who the fiery hell are *you*?"

"I'm the agent in charge of this operation."

"I heard that sound earlier," Matt said. "I thought she was just enjoying her ice cream."

"Wait just a freaking minute. You thought *I* was slurping like a dog? How dare you."

Matt scowled. "Look. This is serious. Obviously, you've ditched your tracer. How do you expect us to

146

keep you safe if you don't cooperate?"

I whistled for Bear. A minute later, he bounded into the room. I pointed at Matt. "Bear, guard." My dog rushed at Matt. His attack bark thundered off the sloping ceiling.

Matt looked totally startled. "Hey, buddy." He held out his wrist.

Bear hit Matt's knee with his shoulder once, twice, three times, until he pushed him against the wall.

"Bear, quiet," I said. "Hold." He stopped barking, but didn't move.

Matt held out his hand again and stepped forward. "Hey, we're buddies. Remember?"

My dog took Matt's wrist in his mouth but did not clamp down. He nudged Matt with his shoulder, pushing him back again. "Look," Matt said, glaring at me, "this is ridiculous." Again, he stepped forward. Bear still held Matt's wrist, and with a low growl, he butted Matt's knees, hard this time. Matt stumbled back against the wall.

"Good boy, Bear. See you later, Matt." I gloated as I walked out of the room. "Let me know when you need a potty break." I stomped toward the stairs.

Chapter Sixteen

I stomped down the stairs from the attic. Thank God I could count on Bear. I finally understood that sappy old saying, "My heart swelled with pride." It did. I was so proud of Bear that a lump rose in my throat and my heart thumped a little harder.

Who needed Matt anyway? He of the six-pack abs and enchanting dimples. With just one touch, he'd made me tingle from top to bottom. And he liked me— as bait. Sweet.

Jake clumped down the stairs after me. At the bottom, he laid a fatherly hand on my shoulder. He waited until I turned around to face him. "You've got some kind of spunk, kiddo. But until Bear gives you back your tracer, you're stuck with me."

"So, tell me, who's this Devine character you're waiting for?"

"He's a very dangerous man, Heather. It's better you don't know."

I pulled myself up tall, ready to tell him what a coward he was, but something stopped me. It was his tone of voice, laced with care. He sounded just like my brother.

He turned gruff. "Look, it's been a long, tough day, and you have every right to be angry, but this isn't a James Bond movie. A trick like that could get you killed."

It shocked me to see how tired he looked. And then I really looked at him. The dim light of the hallway threw the lines on his face into shadow, making them deeper than usual. Maybe he had caved, but he didn't like it. He had tried. He had stuck up for me.

I whistled for Bear. As my dog pattered down the stairs, a smile spread across Jake's craggy face. Obviously, he approved of Bear. He rubbed his head; waited while I removed the tracer from Bear's kerchief and put it back on. Then, he touched my shoulder. "Hang in there, kiddo," he said. Maybe he approved of me, too, or at least what my dad called my spunk.

Like a tidal current, the sting of Matt's betrayal started to ebb. I wasn't ready to forgive him; not yet, not while I was still flayed and bleeding. But in the deepest recesses of my soul, I knew he was trying to do the right thing.

Jake went back upstairs to deal with the devil, and I turned into the kitchen. Jordy looked up from a large spoon heaped with ice cream. "You're just in time. We're dishing up the rest."

I'd opened a door into another world: a safe, sane, normal world. I slid back into my chair. Bear settled at my feet. Cold, sweet, creamy strawberries melted seductively in my mouth. Suddenly, I didn't want to be anywhere but there, at this generous table with Sam, Penny, Mary, and the boys.

We played poker and Yahtzee until long after midnight, and when I finally climbed into bed, my shoulder still felt warm where Jake's hand had rested. I cupped my hand over that spot and slept long and hard.

By the time I got up the next morning, Mary was in the kitchen. The Koffee Hour was on the radio, volume

149

turned low, and she was on the phone. "I'm calling in," she said, taking a chair at the table.

"What's up? Trying to sell a couple of boys?"

She grinned, then introduced herself to the radio audience and announced the memorial service for Mariella. "... Monday evening, around seven o'clock on the patio beside Sam's Inn." She caught my eye, held up crossed fingers, and pulled in a deep breath. "Some of you may be wondering how she died. There have been rumors, and I, myself, wondered if she might have been the victim of foul play, but Sheriff O'Toole assures me that her death was accidental. If you knew Mariella, please join us in remembering her on Monday." She hung up the phone.

I stared at her. "What on earth was that about?" My voice rose. "Mariella was clearly dead before she hit the water, of massive blows to the head. Why do you have to lie?" My pulse raced. "Don't tell me. I already know. It's all part of the plan." How could I have forgotten, even for a few hours, that to the men in Sam's attic, I was merely a chunk of bait?

That included Matt. In the bright light of day, the truth stared me in the face. I'd been a fool for letting myself think he cared about me.

Mary asked, "What are you talking about?"

"Things are getting way too weird around here." No matter how hard I tried, I couldn't summon up a single ounce of grace. "Matt and the guy the boys call Smiley are up there in Sam's attic piping a tune, and Jake is dancing to it." I got up, grabbed a sponge and started wiping up milk spills on the counter.

Mary looked at me as if I'd come unglued. "Jake told me that he wants to allay fears, and that he wants to lull Mariella's killer into thinking he got away with it. Then, maybe he'll let down his guard and slip up somehow. It makes sense. My dad caught a guy once because he got drunk and told the bartender he did it."

"No, here's the deal . . .." I clamped my hand over my mouth.

It was Mary's turn to stare. "What?"

I wrapped my fingers around the tracer. "I can't tell. I promised."

She came and stood beside me as I scrubbed furiously at the already-clean counter top. "What on earth are you talking about?" She put a hand on my arm. "You didn't just go to the restroom at Sam's last night, did you? You were gone a long time. What did you do? What's going on?"

I put a finger on my lips to shush her. It took only a second to remove my locket. I wrapped it in a thick yellow towel, stuffed it into a big old bean pot, and put the lid on. I set the pot beside the radio and turned the volume up. I leaned close to her ear and whispered, "Let's go out on the deck. That isn't just a tracer. I have no privacy at all. They can see what's in my cereal bowl. They listen to me in the bathroom, for God's sake. They can hear every fart. For all I know, they can smell it, too. I have never been so totally invaded and insulted."

Mary nudged me out of the kitchen. "No kidding," she whispered. She led the way through the living room. "I thought it looked pretty fancy for little old Sterling County."

Neither of us bothered to keep the screen door from banging shut as we walked out onto the deck. We sat at the picnic table, side by side like conspirators on a park bench in Leningrad during the cold war, each of us ostensibly reading a newspaper or feeding the pigeons, watching to see if anyone approached, waiting for the right moment to trade our secrets.

I told her everything, starting with waking up the first morning and watching two black shadows club the water-skier to death, and how they shot their way into the cabin and chased me the night I was hurt. I finished with what I'd heard in Sam's attic the night before. When I told her that some guy named Devine was supposed to come back and do me in, Mary's face blanched.

"See?" I said. "You're involved in this plot without your knowledge or consent. I think it's dreadful that Matt and Jake think you don't need to know. Having me stay here could be dangerous for you and the boys."

She was quiet for a moment or two. Then she said, "I don't think we need to worry about that. My dad always said contract killers are into precision."

"So, what's precise about going out water skiing and running over the guy with a boat? Sticking a knife between his ribs would have been faster and a heck of a lot quieter."

"True." She stared out at the lake for a minute. "Actually, that sounds more like something a serial killer might do. Some of them really get off on toying with their victims—having a sense of power over life and death."

Mary chewed on a fingernail—a habit she said, over and over, she was trying to break. She wasn't as cool as she was attempting to sound. "When Dad worked homicide in San Francisco, he spent years trying to track down a murderer who was both a hit man and a serial killer. Maybe this Devine person is one of those, too."

"Jake should have told you what's going on."

Mary reached over, curled her hand around mine, and squeezed it gently. "Nobody's interested in me and the boys. You're the only one that matters."

I couldn't think what I would do without her support. "There's no way I'm going to feel good about dragging you into this, but thank you." I tried to believe everything would be okay.

After a minute, she said, "My father would say the less we know the better. That way, we'll act normally, see. That's probably why Jake hasn't told us."

"Even if he has a good reason, it's unfair. And it's not just Jake. Matt's in it, too, and I'm pissed as hell at him. He thought I'd fall into a swoon because he told me he wanted to meet me. He thought I'd trust him because he pretended to admire my performances at the theater. He even said he has season tickets. I almost fell for it, too."

Mary smiled. "I wouldn't be at all surprised to see him at the theater. I think he's a closet thespian. He was always in our school plays. He seemed to get a kick out of wearing a tattered old bathrobe and tying a dish towel on his head at Christmas. Nearly every year, he acted the part of Joseph."

I should have known she'd defend him.

"I get it, though. You feel like Matt is using you." Mary stared out at the lake for a minute and then seemed to decide on something. "No matter what, I trust Jake and Sam to keep us all safe, and this is a good place for you to be. It's small. There aren't that many people, and we know most of them. Where else would they be able to see everyone who comes and goes?"

She was right, but it didn't make me feel better.

At that moment, the boys ran up the steps to the deck, Jordy holding Bear's leash. "Actually," I said, "we'd all be safer if Jordy had a dog like Bear."

"Yeah, Mom. When Dad's away, you're always scared we'll get burgled."

Mary grinned. "As if you need Heather's help."

She deserved it. She *would* stick up for Matt.

"Sam says it's going to storm," Travis said. "He wants us to see if the boats are all tied up properly, but we need a sandwich first."

"Okay. You know where stuff is." Mary waved a hand toward the kitchen. "Sam's right about the weather. It's getting really sticky."

We both looked up. Out over the lake, a line of clouds marched across the sky, tall and white, brilliant against the blue. Already, the wind was picking up. The storm would soon be unleashed. I wondered when the other storm, the one brewing in Sam's attic, would begin. It would take more than a sandwich to cope with that one. I had to admire Mary's determination. I even felt a faint glimmer of regard for myself and my role in stopping the bad guys.

After a couple minutes, the boys trooped back across the deck, sandwiches in hand. They bounced down the stairs and headed for the dock, where a dozen runabouts were fastened loosely to the cleats. From our perch, we watched them go from boat to boat, putting down extra fenders and tightening lines. Before they finished, the sky darkened and wind came rushing down the lake, setting the water in motion, quickly building white caps.

On the sandy beach just off to our left, mothers of the little kids gathered towels, water wings, and children. A sudden gust flipped over a bright yellow float, and it skidded up onto the lawn. The kids turned their backs and yelled in pain as sand whipped against their bare legs. Everyone started toward shelter, kids crying and mothers coaxing them to hurry. Another gust toppled lawn chairs at the edge of the water, and the yellow float rolled awkwardly across the grass, flopping like a beached fish.

Two small boats plowed by, both of them overloaded with teenagers, none of whom were wearing life vests, running in close to shore, headed toward town. Waves crashed against the dock, sending geysers of water high in the air. The temperature had dropped ten degrees in as many minutes. A dust devil swirled up a funnel of leaves and twigs and dirt and flung the debris at us.

Mary shielded her eyes with her hand. "That's not very friendly." Blinking, we picked up T-shirts and wet towels, which were blowing off the railing.

The boys returned as I grabbed our coffee cups off the picnic table. I held the door open with my foot and everybody went in, including Bear. As if a little wind would damage him. Up-lake, thunder rolled. We gathered around the table in the screened porch and Mary shuffled a deck of cards. "Poker anybody?"

We were bluffing, keeping our poker faces on, and bidding outrageously when, accompanied by the crisp scent of ozone, the storm broke overhead. In a matter of minutes, lightning, thunder, and huge drops of rain were followed by hail, small and soft at first, then harder and larger until they were as big as moth balls.

Putting our cards face down on the table, we scrambled to stand at the screens and watch. Soon the lawn was more white than green. Under the black belly of the thunderclouds, the lake was a dull, dark menace crested with foam.

Travis pointed at the dock. "Look. There go Sam and Matt." Shoulders hunched against the hail, the men hurried across the slick wood planks. "They're getting pounded. Bet that hurts." They climbed into Matt's boat. Sam untied the lines while Matt started the motor.

"Someone must be in trouble." Mary bit a fingernail as she scanned the lake.

Turning at the end of the dock into open water, Matt followed the center of the storm as it romped on ahead. Sam stood beside him. Both held onto the top of the windscreen, as if scanning the lake ahead.

"Those waves are dangerous." Mary put her hands on her hips. "I hope they know what they're doing."

"Sam?" Jordan snorted. "Sam knows everything about the lake."

Pitching and rolling, the boat disappeared off to the right. We sat back down to our poker game. Minutes later, the hail stopped. Rain, pushed sideways by the wind, drummed on the cabin roof. Travis had just dealt me a pair of aces and three jacks when a small, sporty, black car pulled up beside Mary's cabin.

A tall, slim woman in a long red cape with a hood got out of the car and hurried up onto the deck. "Knock, knock," she called.

Mary jumped up to open the door for her. "How are you, Simone? Get in here before you drown."

I had met Simone Rideau a couple of times before. She and her husband operate a winery and a small, expensive restaurant on the north shore, across the lake from Sam's. Tall and model-thin, she wears clothes the way I wish I could. That afternoon, her gray hair was swept back in a French knot, leaving her large dark eyes to dominate her face. "I heard you on the Koffee Hour this morning, and decided I'd better drive over and talk to you."

"What is it?" Mary asked. We all sat down.

"It may be nothing, but the Friday before last, we took some guests up to the head of the lake on the mail boat, just for the day, to see the sights."

The day of the murder in my cove. The day I got hurt. The last day anyone saw Mariella. My chest tightened. Mary and I exchanged glances.

"On the way back down, a youngish man got on at the fire lookout station. Now, you know, there's nothing there, but he hadn't even a day pack with him, and he wasn't on the boat on the way up that morning. I thought that was curious, so although I felt I was being a bit of a busybody, I watched where he got off. He debarked at the trail head, you know, at the parking lot where the road ends. Someone was waiting for him in a pretty fancy sports car."

I gasped. I felt the blood drain from my face.

"Was it red?" Mary asked.

"It was."

"Oh, man," Jordy said. "You have to tell the sheriff."

Only Simone remained calm. "It's not a common sort of car around here, is it?" She scanned our faces. "Do you think it could be the one that young woman died in?"

"For sure," Travis and Jordy chorused.

It all fit. The man Simone saw could have been one of the killers. He would have had time to take the boat up-lake and scuttle it. Then all he had to do was swim ashore and wait for the mail boat to come by.

"What did he look like?" I asked.

Simone stared into the distance for a moment. "In a word, medium: medium brown hair, about six feet tall, medium build. He wore khaki shorts, a plain black T-shirt, and a baseball cap pulled down low, and he kept off to himself."

Frowning, Simone stood. "I didn't get a good look at the driver of the car, either, but in a way, he resembled Bill Harlan. Not that it was Bill, of course. Just someone about his size." She took her cape off the hook where Mary had hung it, swirled it around her shoulders, and pulled the hood up. "I hope I haven't kept this to myself too long, but I didn't put it together until I heard you on the Koffee Hour."

I stared at Simone's back as she left. Charlie could be described as medium. But I couldn't picture him without his leathers and fringes. I could barely breathe. Had she seen the phantom Devine?

She was halfway down the steps when I saw Matt's boat returning, splashing through the waves. Behind the boat a tow line stretched back to a craft that looked like a pregnant sardine can with one pointy end. It pitched murderously in the waves, to the point I wondered what kept it from rolling over.

Jordan pressed his forehead against the screen. "Holy shit!" His head whipped around and he looked over his shoulder at his mother. "Cow, I mean. Holy cow."

"You'd better," Mary said. "I don't want to hear

that again, young man."

"Mom, this is the extreme. Come see for yourself." He darted to the coat hooks. "Come on, Travis." Grabbing his yellow slicker, he started outside. Travis was only steps behind. Bear begged to go with them, but I wasn't letting him out of my sight.

Mary called, "Put your hoods up, you two."

"Yeah, we will." Travis obeyed while Jordan turned his face up to the rain and held his tongue out.

"Are you thinking what I'm thinking?" Mary asked, looking as troubled as I felt. "The man Simone saw on the mail boat must have been one of the killers."

"Possibly. And the guy who picked him up might have been the other one."

"Neither of them sounds like Charlie."

"Remember, he has a whole gang of thugs at his disposal. Actually, Simone might not have seen the killers at all. She could have the seen any two of them."

"True," Mary agreed. "It's impossible to know."

"Whatever is going on," I said, "it's big. Matt and Smiley wouldn't be hanging out in Sam's attic with all that surveillance gear if it wasn't."

Mary nodded. "We all need to stick together."

"Yeah, like pigeons in a shooting range."

For a minute, she was quiet. Then she said, "We can count on Jake and Sam to work it all out."

A big part of me couldn't help thinking that Mary was burying her head in the proverbial sand. But with all my might, I hoped she was right.

She went to the window, pressed her forehead against the screen, and peered at the lake. "That's got to be Matt's friend's sub. If he is planning to go down in that piece of tin, he's gone right over the edge."

Travis and Jordan had skidded across the lawn on melting hailstones, leaving ski tracks behind. They slowed down when they came to the dock, which was still as white as Christmas, and scuffed along, all the way out to the end where it branched into a tee.

The sub was tiny, bigger than a sardine can, of course, but not much, and the same color. It looked totally un-seaworthy. Matt cut a wide arc around one arm of the tee and headed in. Rocking and rolling, the sub trailed along behind him. In the dome that rose out of the deck, there were three portholes, a very small one on each side and a slightly larger one in front. There was a round hatch on top.

"Talk about claustrophobia," Mary said. "Imagine being underwater in that. What is going to keep it from collapsing under the pressure? I expected him to have better sense."

Sam stood in the stern, watching the tow line. When Matt stopped, Sam pulled the line in, and as the sub drifted closer, stuck his foot out to keep it from bumping into Matt's boat. Jordy slipped and slid to the sub and pushed against the dome to fend it off the dock. It dipped and bobbed like a cork.

The hatch opened just as a ray of sunshine broke through the clouds. It landed on the sub and its skipper, a spotlight straight from heaven. She had long dark hair gathered with a clip at the back of her neck, and there was no doubt in my mind from the first second I saw her that she was gorgeous. She braced her arms on the rim of the hatch, pushed herself up, and sat there, one leg in and one out. Matt leaped out of his boat and charged back to the sub, slipping and nearly falling into the lake in his haste.

Mary took a look through the binoculars. "I know her. She was in my fifth-grade class with Matt. She was always cute, but now she's beautiful. That periwinkle jacket is the perfect color." She handed me the glasses. "They must have remained friends all these years."

As I lifted the binoculars, I tried to tell myself I didn't care if Matt's friend was female. And beautiful. She had dark hair and eyes, highly colored cheeks, and a big wide smile.

I felt Mary looking at me, so I did my best to sound nonchalant. "He told me his friend's name was Paul."

She reached out to take the glasses back. "Her name is Paulette, and she hates it, or she did when she was little and wanted to be called Paul. I can't believe she's not seasick."

Matt tied the sub to the dock.

I hoped she'd barf on his shoes.

"Her dissertation is on alternative energy systems," I said. And she has legs that go on forever, in very skinny jeans. I smiled as if I wasn't even a tiny bit jealous. "Very ambitious. It will be fun to meet her." About as much fun as getting new braces.

She took Matt's hand, hopped onto the dock, and threw her arms around him. He lifted her feet off the ground and swung her around in an exuberant circle—two circles.

I would definitely call her Paulette.

Chapter Seventeen

Late afternoon sunshine followed the storm. Relishing the fresh, pure air, Mary and I dried off a couple of deck chairs, plunked down, and watched folks emerge from their cabins, wearing sweaters over their tees. Most joined Travis and Jordan on the dock, where they examined Paulette's sub and undoubtedly told her how brilliant she was.

Matt wrenched himself away from the excitement of the sub and its beautiful skipper to cross the hailstone-speckled lawn to Mary's cabin. With every step he took, I felt more alone and empty. Clearly, periwinkle was his favorite color. When he came up the stairs to the deck, Mary touched my arm and slipped into the cabin, leaving us alone.

"I came to ask for your help," he said, not quite meeting my eyes. "We plan to take the sub down in your cove, as you know, and look for your water-skier."

"You mean Mariella's boyfriend. Your colleague. Ken Lagazo."

He shook his head, "We can't be certain."

We stared at each other for several beats before he said, "Paul would like you to come along. She thinks some local knowledge might be useful."

Our last encounter, that night in Sam's attic, still burned. I was not about to forgive him for convincing Jake to wait for a professional killer to come back and do me in. "Better local knowledge than live bait." I tried to sound breezy and bright, but my mouth felt stiff. I sounded stiff.

He gazed at me for a moment, opened his mouth to speak, and then closed it again. He shifted his weight from one foot to the other. "Please, Heather. I'd like you to come."

"Fine. I have nothing to do but rest my liver." I hadn't used that tone of voice since I was thirteen.

"Okay. I'll come by for you in the morning."

We stood looking at each other for another long, uncomfortable minute. I didn't offer him a chair, a glass of iced tea, or anything. Finally, he turned and left.

Later, when Mary and I sat down for dinner with the boys, all they could talk about was the sub and Paulette whom, of course, they called Paul. For a change, Travis had the most to say. "She had to surface during the storm. One of the portholes was leaking."

Lovely. If it leaked when it was ten feet deep, what would happen under three or four atmospheres of pressure?

"She was afraid it would blow right in if she didn't get it fixed." Travis waved his arms enthusiastically. "Kah-blooie!"

Jordy's exuberant nod made his cowlick dance. "Yeah, but when she surfaced, she couldn't handle it in the waves, so Matt had to go rescue her." He looked at me with a crooked little half-grin and a glint in his hazel eyes. I pretended not to notice.

"Yeah." Travis squirted a circle of ketchup onto his hamburger. "Matt took her to the hardware store to buy something to fix it with, the porthole, I mean." He jammed the top of his hamburger bun down onto the meat and clamped slender fingers around it. "She's pretty smart. She built it herself, except her brothers did the welding for her."

I didn't know if I was more jealous because Matt risked getting pounded with hailstones to go to her rescue or because the boys were impressed with someone who roamed around the lake in a home-made mini-submarine. Clearly, they considered me as interesting as the dining room table.

We had fallen into a routine. We all knew our places. We even sat in the same chairs at every meal. I had become a fixture. Paulette made me feel like an old shirt kept around for Saturdays.

"Earth to Heather." Jordan tipped his head to one side and waved a hand in front of me. "I said, why do you get to go?"

I jerked myself back. "Go where?"

"In the sub. Matt says they're going to look for the guy who was driving the sports car because he must have got out, but he didn't turn up anywhere."

While I wanted to yell, *Matt's lying his snug little ass off*, I pretended nonchalance. "They need me because I know the lake. Paulette can only drive the sub." Pointing out her limitations felt good. Sneaky, but good nevertheless.

Jordy snorted. "I could go. I know the lake." He took a big bite. His ruddy, freckled cheeks worked vigorously.

The boys' hamburgers were gone in minutes, and they carried their plates to the kitchen before Mary and I finished eating. While we lingered over mint tea and watched the fading light turn the hills on the north shore purple and then dark blue, the boys banged and splashed in the kitchen until the dishes were done. Then they headed back down to the dock where Paulette, still wearing the periwinkle jacket that set off her dark hair and eyes so beautifully, bent over the porthole.

We were going to start at sun-up because Paulette could only stay one day, but it made no sense to go to bed early. The sub looked like what it was: a low-cost student project with a leaky porthole—a nightmare waiting to happen. Sleep seemed too much to expect. The fact that I'd agreed to let Paulette lock me in and dive to the bottom reinforced my brother Tom's theory that I had suffered brain damage at birth.

When at last the boys climbed into bed with their books, Mary and I wrapped ourselves in blankets and went out on the deck, where we listened to the crickets chirping and watched the night sky. The Milky Way hung over us, a dazzling canopy sliced by satellites moving steadily around the globe. We wondered how many other worlds were out there, if any were populated with sentient beings, and whether all species knew love and hate, good and evil, weakness and power. And if they wore pajamas when they went to bed. Finally, we went to bed. I woke up every half hour to worry and to shine my flashlight on my watch.

When the alarm buzzed at around four in the morning, I felt as if I'd spent the night on a red-eye from New York to Seattle—groggy and spaced-out. I pulled sweats on over shorts and a T-shirt, shoved my hair back behind my ears, and then stumbled to the kitchen, where I genuflected in gratitude in front of the espresso machine as it gurgled out a double shot. With shoes in one hand and my steaming cup in the other, I tiptoed through the porch where Bear and the boys were sleeping, slowly opened the screened door enough to squeeze through, and went outside onto the deck.

A heavy dew had beaded up on all the chairs, so I stepped into my shoes without sitting down. I looked out over the quiet dark-blue water. The air felt soft and cool on my face. With a start, I realized the last day I'd been outside at that hour had been the day of the murder. Just as on that morning, predawn light made purple silhouettes of the hills on the opposite side of the lake. A diffuse queasy feeling came over me, and I wanted to run and hide. I wished I had inherited Grandma Garnet's formidable will. She never backed away from anything. Even when Grandpa was dying, she faced losing him and their story-book life together with dignity and grace.

I sipped my coffee, rich and dark, earthy tasting. Grandma Garnet would tell me I needed to trust my heart, that I shouldn't be too concerned about the fact that Matt wouldn't name his employer. And if he altered the truth to suit his needs, then it must be for a good reason. Closing my eyes, I remembered how good it felt when he kissed me. I leaned back against the door frame. I could use another kiss . . ..

A footstep on the wood stair leading up to the deck made me jump. Coffee sloshed over the rim of the cup. Matt came quickly up toward me. In the dim light, I couldn't read his expression, but his voice vibrated with excitement. "Ready to get in the sub?"

"Not." I shook my head to clear the cobwebs. I wiped the coffee off my hand on the seat of my sweats. "I know we need to find the body, but the idea of being closed up in that thing makes me claustrophobic." I sucked in a breath. "Besides, the fish have had ten days to chew on him. I've heard they start nibbling on the soft parts first, like the lips and eyelids, and while I don't blame them for eating the occasional human who comes by, I don't want to see it."

I had to give him credit for hiding his grin. "It sounds as if you've given this some thought," he said, as he started down the steps. "I'm afraid the fish will eat what they want. If it's too gruesome, close your eyes. Paul and I will do the rest." At the bottom of the stairs, he waited for me to catch up, then put an arm around my shoulders and pulled me close. He held up a brown paper sack. "I brought some breakfast for the humans."

I leaned into his solid warmth. He wasn't much taller than my five feet ten but we fit well together. Pressed against him, I felt safe, safe enough to let my feelings out. "I hate having this hanging over me. I hate not knowing for sure who the skier was and why they killed him. I hate looking over my shoulder all the time, wondering who's lurking around, waiting for a chance to do me in."

I was hoping for some hero-type response, but all he said was, "Let's get started. Paul's in the sub already. She's pretty excited. And she swears she's worked out the porthole bugs."

My stomach tightened. "Sure, with hardware store glue." I wanted to turn around. My warm, cozy bed was calling.

"Don't worry. The guy in the store says they sell a lot of that glue, so it hasn't been sitting on the shelf forever. It's nice and fresh."

His grin drew me in—for a second—but I prevailed and pulled away from him. "Don't tease me."

167

"It'll be fine." He pulled me back. "Actually, the portholes are soldered in. But there was a tiny gap on one side. That's what she fixed."

"You make it sound like we're just going out for a fun little jaunt."

"From Paul's perspective, it's an important test. This will prove she's built a useful submersible that runs on a renewable energy source and doesn't pollute."

"So, it's all about Paulette."

He stepped back. "It's more than that, and you know it. Without a body, we don't have a case."

"Exactly. The only reason I'm going."

He paused, looked at me in the dim light. "You certainly are prickly this morning."

"Sorry." *Not.*

"It's okay."

We continued across the lawn in silence, our elbows occasionally bumping together. I was glad for that. I wanted him to be there, sturdy and steady. Stepping onto the dock, I sipped my coffee. "Want some?" I held out my cup, a peace offering.

"Thanks. I've been thinking about ripping it out of your hand." Stopping, he cupped his warm hand around my cool fingers and drank from the same side of the mug. I watched as he put his lips right where mine had been and my knees went all quivery. He took one sip, then another. "Mmmm. That's good." Slowly, he took his hand away. Shifting the sack of groceries, he put his arm around my shoulders again and we continued down the dock. When he spoke, his tone sounded reflective. "I need to talk to you later."

Out of the corner of my eye, I saw Paulette standing on the bow of her pregnant little sardine can, looking at us. Was that why Matt let go of me just then?

As I stepped onto the foredeck, she untied the lines. "Jump in, Heather."

I sat on the cool damp top with my feet dangling down into the sub and slid in through the hatch. My feet touched a seat, and I stepped down onto the floor. My head and shoulders stuck out. I was in a tube, sort of like a soup can that wasn't much more than four feet in diameter. It tapered slightly up to the top. The seat was just a wood board that ran from side to side behind the two tiny portholes. In front of it, in the center, a red vinyl soda-fountain stool had been fastened to the floor. In front of that was the forward porthole above a small instrument panel.

I sat on one end of the bench and made myself as small as possible while Matt followed me in and sat on the other side. Then Paulette slid down. Matt and I both leaned back against the hull while she crouched between us and closed the hatch, shutting out most of the light as she tightened down the turnbuckles.

I knew by the thick black goop encircling my porthole that I had the leaky one. I took a deep breath and let it out slowly. I was sealed in a soup can welded to the top of a sardine can and was breathing dank, mildew-infested air.

Would that glue really hold once we got down to three or four atmospheres of pressure? It was kind of dark in there, too. And it was my own fault. If I had just said no to Alex instead of running away, I'd be at home, safe in my own bed.

Paulette settled her cute little buns onto the round swivel stool. I wondered whether one of her brothers had cut the legs off short and bolted it down for her or if she'd done that herself. She turned and smiled. "Ready?"

I nodded.

A faint red light came on above the control panel. The motor hummed. Paulette gripped what looked like a video-game joystick attached to a tablet computer. As she pushed the stick to one side, we glided silently away from the dock. She pushed it forward, and we went ahead. From somewhere in the distant past, a Bible verse popped into my head, "Like a lamb to the slaughter . . .."

That was how I felt. I had to wonder how long it would be before the three of us used up all the oxygen. "Do you have compressed air on board?" I asked. Someone had to make sure we'd keep on breathing.

In front of me, her ponytail bobbed up and down. "Yes. Don't worry." She flipped a switch and a fan wafted cool air down the back of my neck. "And if anything goes wrong, I can divert the air into a couple of bladders. They will inflate on the deck and take us to the surface. In the meantime, I have filters to draw out the moisture from our breath. It gets wet enough in here just from condensation."

Whoop-dee-freaking-doo. The woman thought of everything.

We bobbed along on the wrinkled surface of the lake until we were clear of the dock. To my surprise, I liked the peculiar rocking motion of the stubby craft. Just as I decided things might be okay, I saw water beginning to inch up over my porthole. At first, it was light green in color, but soon it changed to blue-gray. As the light in the cabin diminished, the little red light above the instrument panel seemed brighter.

Paulette glanced at me over her shoulder. "Matt doesn't want anyone to see which way we go, so I'll level off just below the surface at ten feet."

Ten feet. Cool. I can handle ten feet. "How can you see where you're going?"

"Can't. I'm on instruments."

I peered over her shoulder. The control panel looked rudimentary: compass, knot meter, depth gauge, a bubble level, a small GPS screen, now blank. Doubt clutched at my throat. I swallowed. "How many times have you been down?"

She chuckled. "Five. Never more than fifty feet, though. Something has always cut it short. But there can't be any more bugs." Her voice carried a jaunty ring. "Today will be the real test."

Matt squeezed my hand. "Cut it out, Paul. You're making the passengers nervous."

"Here are my calculations." She held up a clipboard which had been resting on her lap. "I have to navigate by compass for now. At this speed we'll enter your cove in seventeen minutes. When we get there, I'll come up until the GPS antenna is out of the water. We'll be able to see right where we are and with you looking at the map, Heather, we should be able to find the spot where the water-skier went down. To conserve energy, we need to get as close as possible before we dive. We'll descend by circling at a constant rate until we find the grid the divers laid out. Then all we have to do is find where the cliff drops off and go on down."

I considered telling them to take me back to Sam's, but what the heck? I had nothing else to do that day, and I wasn't going to get another chance to risk my life this way. I started counting the minutes, trying to guess exactly when we'd get to our cove.

Paulette said, "I'll be more likely to get us there if I don't starve."

Matt opened the grocery sack and pulled out plastic bottles of orange juice. Next, he split open a crusty roll and cut a wide wedge of Brie with a pocket knife. Balancing the cheese on the roll, he handed it to Paulette, then offered his knife to me. I shook my head at the Brie but took a roll.

Paulette juggled her food with one hand and controlled the sub with the other. Every few seconds, I checked all three portholes, especially mine, for signs of leakage, but the seals held. Then I glued my gaze back on the compass and bubble level, mentally holding the craft steady, making sure we remained upright and on course.

The captain brushed crumbs off her shirt. "If my calculations are correct, we're at the mouth of your cove, Heather. I'll go up closer to the surface, until the GPS antenna is out of the water." She pointed at the screen in front of her. "If you would watch now, the map will appear and you can tell me if I need to turn one way or the other."

I leaned forward. The compass began to rotate. More light came in the portholes, and soon the GPS screen lit up, showing the shoreline below our cabin. The sub looked like a tiny little sesame seed moving steadily toward the center of the bay. I guided Paulette as best I could, but it was difficult. I couldn't find the landmarks I was able to see from the cabin.

When I said I thought we were where the water-skier disappeared, the sub pitched down. Instantly, the light faded. The sun would not reach this part of the lake for a while yet. Soon, we floated in a silent black abyss. I felt as if I were tumbling into a void. I gripped my roll so hard it became a little lump in my palm. In the dim red light, the compass slowly spun through north to west to south to east then north again. As we began another revolution, I divided my attention between the compass and the depth gauge. Just as Paulette said, we were descending at a steady pace, passing thirty feet, then forty, fifty, and on to ninety.

"How do you do that?" I asked.

"Just have to trust the instruments," she answered quietly.

I stared out the forward porthole, into the darkness. When we reached one hundred feet, Matt said, "We should be close."

She flipped a switch and a light beamed into the water. Tiny motes floated in the water, like dust in a sunbeam. But there was nothing else to see. Silently, we all peered out. Paulette slowed the rate of descent and turned in a wider circle.

The sub creaked and popped and I ran my fingers along the wall under the portholes. Not even a drop of water had seeped in via my porthole, but a trickle oozed from the one by Matt's head.

"It's okay," he said, taking my hand. "Don't worry."

A couple of minutes passed. "I wish I could see that grid," Paulette said. For the first time, her voice held a note of tension. "We're going to waste too much energy if we don't find it soon."

I took a deep breath, leaned forward to peer over Paulette's shoulder, and willed the yellow rope grid to appear, but the sub's light was puny in all that darkness.

"We should be deep enough," Paulette said. "Matt, are you sure your depth gauge was reading accurately that day you dove here?"

"It's pretty accurate."

"In that case," I said, "we're not close enough to shore. Better go straight south. It will get shallower, and the bottom will show up. Then we can find the grid."

She turned until the compass read one hundred eighty degrees.

Another minute passed. I kept my gaze on the light beam. At last, a length of yellow rope caught my eye. "There! See that?"

Matt rubbed a hand up and down my back, leaving a warm trail that reminded me how chilly I'd become. I didn't care. The only thing that mattered was finding the body. Now that we were there, I didn't want to be anywhere else.

"Whew." Paulette was already turning back toward deeper water. "Good directions, Heather. Here we go." We turned around, descended a little farther, and almost at once, came to the edge of a cliff. It fell straight down, as if it had been whacked off by a giant cleaver.

"Perfect," Matt said. "We had to abandon the search right here."

Paulette turned the sub to parallel the face of the cliff. "I'll set up a slow descent. We'll go back and forth a little way in each direction."

On my side, a light came on, aimed out against the rock wall. I wiped condensed moisture off the glass with my sleeve and cheek to cheek, Matt and I pressed our faces to the tiny porthole. Gliding soundlessly along beside an eerie, barren slope, we might have been exploring another planet. It seemed to be an enormous space, partly because the brown rock sucked up all the light. It was like searching an abandoned dungeon by the light of a birthday candle.

There were lots of fissures and cracks, but we couldn't see a place big enough to hold a body. No flat spots to land on. We turned around. Matt's light came on and mine went out. I leaned across to his porthole, and in the meager light, I saw that the trickle of water was now a steady little stream. I gasped. Matt put his arm around me. "It's okay," he said softly. "I promise, the glass will not blow out, no matter what."

I tried to believe him. But I tensed every time the walls of the sub crackled and popped. I nestled against his reassuring warmth. Every half-minute, we switched back and forth and descended another ten to fifteen feet, as if we were following an old mountain highway.

At a little over two hundred feet, the landscape changed. Matt touched Paulette's shoulder. "Lots of rocks now. Looks like there was a landslide and it all came to rest here. Good place to look."

I strained to see. Boulders of all shapes and sizes, some as big as a pickup truck, cast shadows that tricked my eyes. "Can you slow down?"

Paulette obliged. "We're low on battery power. I didn't think we'd suck it up so quickly, but it's taking a lot to keep the lights on. In seven more minutes, we'll be forced to go up. I'll have to recharge, and that will take most of the day."

"Essentially, it's now or never," Matt said. "We have to find it. Find him." Water was now pouring in his porthole. Matt pulled his sweatshirt off, folded it up, and pressed it against the bottom of the glass. "We are not going up now," he told me. "Just keep looking. This will be a great story to tell our grandchildren."

I couldn't speak, or even think.

Paulette shut off all the lights except the forward one. Matt and I leaned over her shoulders. She angled the sub back and forth, shining the light as best she could into holes and crevices. Four minutes went by. Three minutes left. Two. We all bargained silently for more time.

And then I caught a reflected glint. "Wait, Paulette, stop. Go back."

Matt gave me more room. "What is it?"

"A tiny gleam, something metallic. There, again."

"I'll go in closer." The sub swayed as Paulette drove it right up against the rocks. Without warning, a leg filled her porthole, moving up and down. We were so close I saw tiny hairs wave slowly, back and forth. I shuddered. Beyond it, the other leg became visible. I pressed my face against Matt's shoulder.

He stretched forward and put his head right beside Paulette's. "Somebody wanted to make sure he stayed down here. There's a belt with a ton of scuba weights around his waist. That must be what caught your eye, Heather. Can't see his head. His chest is kind of wedged between the rocks. Lucky for us. Otherwise, he might have drifted."

I broke into a clammy sweat. "That's what they were doing when they were leaning over the side. They were putting the weight belt on him, and then they took off his life ring and threw it into the boat." I tried not to look, but stared all the same at the legs. The lake is very cold at that depth. Decomposition was slow, but still, they were gross—puffy and white.

"Now you'll see the true value of this little tub."

Paulette's voice shook. Outside, a spindly mechanical arm unfolded and reached toward the closer foot. It gripped a noose and a coiled line in slender pincers. Twice, it overshot its target. "Oh, man. We're running out of power." She sounded tense. "This has to work."

Matt patted her shoulder. "Take your time. Go slow." He wrung water out of his sweatshirt then pushed it against his porthole and anchored it there with his shoulder. Icy water sloshed about my feet.

I heard the thud of my heart. Paulette tried again. The noose slid over the foot and moved up around the ankle, then past the knee, all the way up to the thigh. "That should do it," Matt said. The arm flexed, pulling the noose tight, cutting into the bloated flesh.

"Yes." A mixture of relief and jubilation sounded in Paulette's voice. "Now, to inflate the marker." A second arm came into view. It held a deflated balloon, which was attached to the other end of the line. A cartridge protruded from the bottom. The first hand came toward it, pincers extended, and grasped a metal ring on the cartridge. In a silent ballet, the arms moved apart again, pulling the ring away.

The buoy inflated and started toward the surface, the line unrolling behind it. "Piece of cake," Matt said.

"Not a moment too soon." Paulette's voice sounded steadier. "Time to go."

We ascended, circling the line, which stretched toward the surface like a long kelp stalk. By the time we reached sixty feet, sunlight filtered through the water, turning it a light green color. I felt I could breathe again. At fifty-five feet, we circled the buoy, an orange globe about the size of a basketball. Paulette grinned over her shoulder. "A major *fait accompli*. Is this a great little sub, or what?" We continued upward.

"You're amazing, Paul." I patted her shoulder. "I can't believe we found him."

"You got us to the right place," she said.

"But the buoy doesn't reach the surface. How will you find it again?"

Matt pressed both hands against the leaking porthole. "We have the GPS coordinates. Plus, we put a non-directional beacon on it. Tonight, after dark, Jake and Sam will come and drag for the buoy. They should be able to haul in the line and retrieve the body."

Paulette said, "*Voilà*. Justice will be served, and we can go up and get warm."

"This needs to be our secret," Matt said. "Can you stay just under the surface?"

"If I turn off all the electronics and just use the compass, and if we go slowly, I might have enough power to get us back."

"If we can make it that far, let's go on past Sam's. I'd like to surface a little closer to town, so it will look as if we were searching for the driver of the car."

Suddenly, I became aware that my ribs hurt like holy heck and my head ached. My feet were soaked and freezing. My heart felt cold and tired and empty. "In other words, we'll lie. We'll lie to Mary. We'll lie to Travis and Jordan."

Matt nodded, his lips clamped together in a line. "If that's how you prefer to think of it."

****

Back at Sam's and frozen to the core, I climbed out of the sub and stepped onto the bleached-white planks of Sam's dock. As if they had popped out of hyperspace, the entire contingent of kids materialized around us before Matt finished tying up. They flung questions at us and clamored to go for a ride.

Paulette sat on the rim of the hatch, one enviably long leg in and one out, holding a miniature bottle of champagne. She grinned at the kids. "This submarine proved totally seaworthy. She passed all her tests. You can help christen her now."

As if nothing under the clear blue sky could ever be wrong, Matt cheered and clapped right along with the kids when the cork popped out and flew high in the air. Bubbles foamed and fizzed as she poured the champagne over the bow of the sub. Everyone joined in, splashing water over the stubby little boat, laughing and talking. Except me.

The party atmosphere was too much—way more than I could handle in one morning. I stood on the fringe of the happy, chattering crowd and looked on. I couldn't connect in any way. I didn't know the man whose body we found, but I felt certain that Matt did. I had pieced together enough of the story to believe that although they may not have met in person, they were working together. I wanted to cry. But Matt looked just as excited as the kids. As far as I could see, finding the body of Ken Lagazo—that had to be who it was— hadn't touched him at all.

In my surreal daze, I saw Jordan's red head show up next to Matt. "Hey, Matt, didja find anything?"

Matt grinned down at him. "Not even an old boot."

"I bet you were looking for you-know-what, weren't you?"

Matt spoke out of the corner of his mouth like a Saturday morning cartoon character. "Dude, I can't keep anything from you, can I?"

Jordan grinned.

Matt glanced over his shoulder at me. For a fraction of a second, he looked grim. Then he looked back at Jordy. With a conspiratorial wink, he landed a playful punch on Jordy's shoulder.

I backed away from the knot of suntanned shoulders and necks. Shit. How could Matt have done that? Why didn't he just say he couldn't talk about what we had done? We had shared an intense and emotional morning in the sub. I had even started to like Paulette, and I respected her knowledge and skill, but now, with each passing second, I felt more distant from both of them. The gap between us widened until I was all alone, as if I were standing on the south rim of the Grand Canyon and they were on the north.

Like a crone drawing her hooded cloak around herself and shrinking away, I started down the dock. A single organism with multiple jabbering mouths, the crowd of kids parted to let me in, gently undulated around me, and gradually expelled me out the other side. My feet whispered across the hot, dry wood. Just before I reached shore, I met a flock of mothers headed out to see the sub, led by Mary, talking and gesturing, a croissant in one hand.

"Hey, Heather." Her tone sounded falsely bright. "The boys are going to ask Paul if she'll take them for a ride, so I'd better get out there." She peered into my eyes and dropped her voice. "How was it?"

"It was darn cold. I need to get warm."

Mary squeezed my hand.

Faking a smile, I glanced at the other moms. "And I have to pee."

Chapter Eighteen

Good old Heather, I groused to myself, part of the morning entertainment. I plodded up to Mary's cabin and turned on the shower. When the hot water was gone, I found my khaki shorts with all the pockets, and my favorite blue-and-cream-striped shirt neatly folded on the end of my bed. With a sigh, I pulled them on. Mary must have done the laundry. She always seemed to know just what to do.

Bear padded after me. As I hung my towel on the rack in the bathroom, I told him, "I think I'll just hook up with men for fun and sex when the whim takes me, like Alex did with me, sort of, don't you know?" In the kitchen, he balanced a doggie treat on his nose until I said "okay" and then snapped it up in one bite. I rubbed his head and gave him another one. Bear's world was pretty straightforward.

Following Dr. Alicia Mendosa's orders about eating small meals, I took a croissant and a glass of milk outside and sat in the sunshine. I had an appointment with her the next day. If there was any luck left anywhere in the universe, she would say my liver had improved enough that I could drive home to my apartment on the top floor of Mrs. Kraski's house in the Wallingford neighborhood. I allowed myself a moment to enjoy the vision of my own little nest, and then reality set in.

This phantom Devine could find me in Seattle—easily, if he was as dangerous as Jake believed he was. And in the city, he would be just another man. Wallingford was full of big, old houses crowded together on narrow lots; home to people of all ages, many of whom walked to the grocery store or the bus stop. Devine could park his car at the shopping area a few blocks away and walk down the street, looking like any other guy coming home from work or going out for an evening stroll.

In the time it takes to blink, he could slip up the steps from the street and through the gate with the wisteria hanging over it, and he'd be in Mrs. Kraski's narrow side yard where no one would see him. Then he would climb the stairs to my apartment and do me in. In less than five minutes, he would walk away again. Mary was right. Even if Alicia said my liver was totally fine, I couldn't go home. Not yet. Not until Devine showed up and they carted his ass off to jail.

I said "om" a few times and did some deep breathing to quell the tightness in my chest, and then I went through what had become my mantra: The resort was small. Nearly everyone came year after year. Strangers really stuck out. Sam, Jake, Matt, and the other guy in Sam's attic, Smiley, were on guard, watching for him. They would catch him before he could get to me.

Maybe Devine wouldn't show up, and then what? No one knew for sure that he would. It was conjecture, really, based on the idea that if he wanted to maintain his reputation, he wouldn't leave a job unfinished. I could see the logic. If you go to the trouble of hiring a high-end killer, you expect to get your money's worth.

So, if word got around that he botched part of his job and the only witness was still alive, then, poof! His reputation, and therefore, his income, would be gone in a puff of smoke. He would come all right. The only question was when.

I said "om" a bunch of times and repeated "my heart beat is slow and steady" until I could breathe normally again. Exhausted, feeling as worn as an old inner tube, I stared at my plate. I had eaten my croissant without tasting it. There was only one thing to do. I went inside and found another one, a large one laced with chocolate this time, and flopped into a lounge chair on the deck. After all, if Devine had his druthers, I wouldn't need a healthy liver.

Above me, the branches of the old pear tree swayed softly. They reminded me of the legs moving up and down in the dim light of the sub. I had clung to the theory that Charlie killed both Ken and Mariella in a jealous rage—until that night in Sam's attic, when I heard about Devine. That made the murders look more complicated: planned, professional, and motivated by more than jealousy. I'd heard a rumor that drugs were flowing into Canada via high mountain trails. Lake Sterling was a high mountain lake, and the Canadian border was not that far away.

What if Charlie was running drugs and Ken came to investigate? That had to be it. There must have been some pillow talk between Ken and Mariella. He must have told her he was working under cover, and then Mariella, who never kept anything to herself, spilled the beans to Charlie. Then Devine showed up to help Charlie get rid of Ken.

Omigod. My heart beat faster. If they knew that

Ken was working with Matt, then Matt was on the hit list, too. I sat up straight and gazed at the dock. Paulette hopped in and out of her sub, rigging up solar panels to catch the rays and recharge the batteries. Matt fastened them to the deck with bungee cords. Then, while Paulette adjusted the angle of the collectors, Matt sat on the dock, and like a bigger version of the hovering kids, dangled his feet in the water. He and Paulette laughed and talked and snacked on a bag of chips. I finally got it. I saw what he wanted everyone to see: a carefree guy chatting with a pretty woman. I shivered. It could be that his act was keeping him alive.

Something in the back of my mind started to thump around, like a ghost in a locked box, trying to get out—something about the morning of the murder. For a moment, I almost dredged it up, but then it slipped away from me. I tried and tried to bring it back but couldn't. Whatever it was, it left a black cloud of dread hanging over me. I snapped my fingers. "Bear, come."

He crawled out from under the picnic table and stretched, then padded slowly toward me. I curled my fingers into the hair on his neck. "From now on, you're right beside me twenty-four/seven."

I closed my eyes, dry and scratchy from lack of sleep, and tried to stop my brain from spinning around and around, churning up the same old facts.

The next thing I knew, quiet footsteps sounded on the stairs to the deck. I jerked awake and grabbed for Bear. Mary came and sat on the adjacent lounge. "I've been talking with Penny over at Sam's, and I'd like to hear your thoughts on the service we planned, but shall we have some lunch first?"

The rule about lunch was that everybody made

their own, whenever they wanted to eat it. That day, all four of us plus Bear ended up in the kitchen together, bumping our butts and getting in each other's way, setting up a traffic jam at the knife drawer. I wanted to hug them all and tell them I loved them, but that would have made the boys squirm. They would have accused me of being sappy.

Jordy wanted to know if kids were supposed to come to Mariella's memorial.

Mary put a hand on his shoulder and looked at him intently. "Do you think you want to go?"

He stretched his lips into a false grin. "Did Penny make cheesecake for after?"

Mary smiled. "Penny made four kinds of cookies, but no cheesecake."

Travis stopped spreading peanut butter on his bread and banged the knife down. "I think it's so, like, totally gross that people have a party when someone dies. Like when my friend Josh died, when the truck ran over him on his bicycle, I hated it." His hand shook as he added a spoonful of jam. "I'm not going."

"That's okay. It's not like you really knew Mariella."

"I wouldn't go anyway." Travis scowled. "I can't stand it that everybody tells stories and laughs."

The rainy spring day when we'd said goodbye to Harmony popped into my head. I could see my father's pale gray face above his starched white collar, my mother clinging to his arm, Tom trying to look like an adult, and later, all the people barging into our house and stopping to gush at me. "I know what you mean. When my sister died, I was eight, and I couldn't believe everyone was talking about her as if she was still there and everything was okay."

Travis' eyes were wide, dark, liquid brown. "What happened to her?"

"We were playing on a trampoline at our friend's house and Harmony bounced too high. She flew off and landed on her head. My mom said I should have stopped her, but I couldn't. Not when she jumped that high." Slowly, we all turned back to our sandwiches. "Anyway, after everybody left, Grandma Garnet came up to my room and talked to me. She said God wanted Harmony to live with him, and that was as much of an explanation as I ever got."

We were all quiet as we carried our plates and glasses to the table in the porch and sat down. Then Jordy said, "I don't get it about Mariella. Okay, it's s'posed to be an accident, right? But like, first of all it's not even winter, so the road wasn't icy and he couldn't have skidded off. Second of all, that car was pretty far out there. It had to be going like ninety miles an hour. Third of all, where's the driver? He must have got out and swam away. Besides, man, Mariella must have sat there like a dummy, which she isn't, I mean wasn't. Why didn't *she* get out?" He thought for a minute. "Like I said, I don't get it."

Travis said, "So, her boyfriend was driving too fast. Maybe he was, like, kissing her, and the car went out of control." He continued, his tone full of scorn, "He just saved himself. He should have helped her."

"He could have been in shock. Guys don't do that if they're in shock," Jordy put in. "Remember, Mom, you told us in school about that time some guy went off a bridge at Chappa-quick-dick. I could always remember that name."

Mary's lips twitched. "Chappaquiddick. I'm glad you remember something I taught you."

"What's that?" Travis asked.

"Years ago, a now-dead government official drove off a bridge in the middle of the night and went into the water. He got out, but a young woman was trapped in the car and she died."

Travis' eyebrows went up. "For real?"

Mary nodded.

Jordan chewed on his sandwich. "Just like Mariella's boyfriend, but he didn't show up anywhere."

"Maybe he got mixed up and swam the wrong way or something," Travis said.

"I hope he got a cramp and drowned."

Matt strolled up onto the deck, opened the screen door, and put his head inside. "Save any for me?"

"Help yourself." Mary waved a hand in the direction of the kitchen.

He chuckled. "I've eaten, thanks. I came to tell you Paulette can take these two for a ride when they're ready, and then she's going to head on home."

Jordy jumped up. "Hey, cool. We're ready."

"Not so fast." Mary put a hand on his arm. "Finish your lunch. Sit down, Matt. Want something to drink?"

"Actually, I was hoping for a cup of that great java." With an easy smile, he said, "I know how to make it."

"Great. I'd love some." Mary grinned at him. "Make some for Heather, too."

He headed off toward the kitchen. I noticed the bulge in the back pocket of his shorts. "Jake said Mariella's boyfriend's wallet was in the trunk of the car," I mused out loud. "What does that mean?"

Chapter Nineteen

As long shadows painted the lawn dark green and the evening hush settled on the resort, I wondered what I could possibly wear to Mariella's memorial. My sweats were definitely out. Shorts weren't much better. But that was all I had.

Mary stuck her head out of her bedroom door. "May I offer you this?" She held up a pale blue linen sheath. "I promised myself I'd lose five pounds so I'd look good in it before that hubby of mine gets back, but so far I've gained two. It should fit you pretty well."

The dress had simple, well-mannered lines that skimmed over the rib brace, and the locket looked good with it. That inspired me to hide my fading bruises with makeup, and for the first time in many days, I felt ready to face the world.

By the time Mary was ready to go, the boys had set up the chess board on the table in the porch. Neither of them wanted to go to the service, but Jordy promised to show up for the cookies. I put Bear on the leash and reminded him he was *my* dog.

With Bear obediently at heel, we sauntered over to Sam's patio. Where the popcorn had been on movie night, Penny's coffee maker stood on a round table. The checkered cloth fluttered lazily in the breeze. During the afternoon, Jordy and Travis had helped Sam set up twenty-five or thirty white chairs, the same ones they used for weddings, on the lawn beside the patio. The chairs angled toward the lake, half turned away from the swimming pool and possible distractions.

A few people had gathered near the chairs: a small cluster of high-school girls, the owners of the restaurant where I'd met Mariella, the minister from the old hewn-log church in town. Seeing him in his cassock hit me with a force I had only half expected. Mariella was gone. She was not coming back. We were there to say goodbye. And I shared her peril. My feet slowed.

Mary touched my arm. "Those girls sing a cappella, and offered to come out, so I took them up on it. I'd better go introduce myself." Stiffly, I nodded and watched her hurry ahead. I sat down in the last row of chairs, at the end closest to the patio, Bear beside me. I held his leash with both hands. While the rows filled up, I repeated my mantra and reiterated to myself that everyone looked like they belonged in some way to Sam's Resort or the Key of C Restaurant. Soon Sam stood to thank us all for coming.

The program Mary and Penny had planned moved along at an easy pace. When the a cappella group finished their last hymn, the priest asked for a moment of silent remembrance before he pronounced the benediction. Off to my right, near the coffee urn on the patio, I saw Charlie. My mouth fell open and my heart started to hammer.

He stood there in his leathers and tattoos with his head bowed and hands folded in front of him, his long brown hair tied back with a kerchief around his head, Willie Nelson style. One shiny streak ran from top to bottom of his cheek.

Remorseful? Perhaps. Trying to look as if he loved

her and couldn't possibly have killed her? Maybe.

But the tears on his face reached my heart and touched me in an unexpected way, as did his demeanor, the way he was standing there, patiently suffering. My gut told me he didn't do it. Shocked, blank, unable to resolve the chord struck by his grief, I had to get away to think.

With a start, I realized that the part I dreaded most about funerals had begun. People were standing, stretching, murmuring about how nice a memorial it had been. It was over, officially, and I was supposed to participate by making appropriate social noises. The cold black horror that had been with me ever since I'd seen Harmony lying in her white satin casket gripped me. It was always worst at that moment, when people expected polite, soothing, meaningless words to flow out of my mouth. The first burst of laughter hit me, and I had to go. My plan had been to grab a handful of cookies for the boys and go right up to the cabin. But Charlie was between me and the treats, and no matter what, I wasn't ready to have a conversation with him, so I headed back across the lawn.

"Nice little service." Bill Harlan's voice jolted me back to reality.

I looked around. Shades of lavender and bright pink painted the sky. The evening sun bounced off the lake and lit the dock and boats from behind. My breath caught in my throat. They had turned to silhouettes, like the boat and water-skier I had seen that morning less than two weeks before. I shivered, then felt glad Bill was there. He put a hand on my arm. "You okay?"

I shook my head. "I'm never okay at these things. I've hated them ever since my sister died."

He nodded. "I remember. I can almost see the look on your dad's face when he told my parents what happened, and I remember how my dad's eyes misted up. You had just started coming over to Sterling in the summer, so you were pretty young at the time."

"I was eight," I said. "Tom was twelve."

Bill turned to face me. "I can't imagine what losing one of my kids would be like, or my sister, if I had one. Listen, I brought my boat down. Want to go for a little ride?"

It would be cool on the lake, fresh, calm, and away from all the emotion—heavenly. I could forget for a little while about the legs waving in the underwater current, about Mariella, even about the crazed hit man who was supposed to do me in. "Thanks. I'd like that."

Just as we reached the dock, Sam Fitzpatrick sauntered up. "I have the honor of escorting Heather home tonight," he said. Code for "you're not going anywhere with Bill."

"On second thought," I told Bill, "I promised the boys I'd play poker with them after the service. Sorry."

Shoulders sagging, he stood for a minute, shifted his weight from foot to foot, and then without a word, he headed down the dock.

"Hard to believe it's nearly July Fourth already," Sam remarked, heading toward Mary's cabin. "They'll start loading the barge with fireworks day after tomorrow. It should be a great show."

"The fireworks are always wonderful. I'm looking forward to them." It sounded stupid, stilted and stupid. Mariella was gone. Charlie was crying. Bill remembered about my sister. Everything had gone totally weird and we were making small talk. Things

191

always went psycho at funerals.

Sam moseyed along beside me until we reached Mary's cabin. As he turned to go, he said, "Well, I'll just wander back and see if Penny needs my help."

Bear and I walked up the steps. I turned and looked out over the lake. Wispy magenta clouds had taken over the sky and the night breeze had come up. I loved wearing Mary's little dress, but it was sleeveless, and it didn't quite reach my knees. I shivered. I'd make hot chocolate, and the boys could go over and get a bunch of cookies.

I opened the screen door and went into the porch. The chess set was still on the table, and a few pieces stood off on each side. And then I heard it. Silence. No boys. None of their usual noise. Breathless, I tiptoed to the living room, feeling silly, telling myself they'd gone for the goodies the minute they saw people leaving the service. I just hadn't noticed. The kitchen light was on, casting bright yellow light into the living room. Travis lay on the sofa, sleeping.

"Travis?" He never took naps. I raised my voice a bit. "Travis, where's Jordy?"

He didn't move. I shook his shoulder. He didn't respond. His face looked ghostly under his tan and when I touched his arm, it felt cool. I shook him harder. "Travis, are you all right?" I listened for breathing the way I'd learned in CPR and felt a faint puff of breath on my cheek. He looked awful.

"Jordy!" I ran to the hallway. I looked first in Mary's room, then mine. In between, I glanced into the bathroom. "Jordy!"

Bear pranced back to Travis and stood there watching him. I followed Bear. Again, I shook Travis' shoulder and called his name. He didn't respond. I gasped in a breath to yell for Sam and started outside.

And crashed right into a man standing at the end of the sofa. He wore a baseball cap pulled low over his face and a dark colored windbreaker. One gloved hand clamped over my mouth and the other grabbed my locket. With a quick, hard jerk, he broke the chain, searing the back of my neck. He dropped the necklace on the sofa and shoved it down under the cushions. "Heather Shelton. At last." His hand had a death grip on my jaw, fingertips digging in with vicious strength. "I am Devine." He slipped an arm around my waist and pulled me tight. As my broken ribs grated, pain exploded inside my chest.

Bear's warning rumble turned to a growl.

"Call him off. Quietly. Or he's dead—the kid, too." A long, slender blade flashed in the light from the kitchen. "Your choice." Devine relaxed his hold on my mouth.

I struggled to make my voice firm. "Bear, sit."

He sat for a tiny moment, then stood, fully alert.

"Keep him quiet and keep your mouth shut," he said in a voice that purred with self-satisfaction, "or he's just as dead."

I kicked his shin and tried to drive the heel of my hand up into his nose, the way I'd learned in self-defense class.

He dug a thumb into my shoulder and pressed the nerves so hard my hand went numb and limp. "Surprised?" He chuckled. "I have lots of surprises."

In a flash, I was back on the deck of my cabin. It was early morning, and I was watching two black shadows, one clubbing the water-skier, hitting him over and over. And when the sickening sound of breaking bone stopped, I heard that same laugh, long and low and full of pleasure.

"I'm going to let go of you in a minute," he whispered. "Keep still and keep your voice down. I'll let you guess what will happen if you displease me." Slowly, he relaxed his grip.

"What have you done to Travis?" My voice quavered. "Where is Jordy?"

"I'll show you. Come on. Outside." He looped an arm around my shoulders. "Act nice, like we're going out for an evening stroll, and just in case you don't, my very sharp knife is only three inches from your heart."

I held Bear's collar. "Bastard."

"That wasn't nice." I felt burning pain under my shoulder blade and then a warm trickle down my back. He grinned. "Hurts, doesn't it?"

I held my breath and waited for the pain to ease. There was no way I'd answer.

"Smile. I like going out with beautiful women. And behave. I'd prefer not to kill you yet. The night is young, and I've planned a little diversion, a contest, if you will."

I opened the screen door, crossed the deck, and walked down the stairs. With every step, I felt his body locked to mine, hip to hip, the heat of him at my back.

Everyone was still over at Sam's, on the patio. "It was good of them to gather over there out of the way," he said, grinning down at me. "Made my job easy."

I didn't dare scream for help. I tried to jerk away, but he tightened his grip. "Look," I said, "I'll go wherever you like if you bring Jordan back inside."

He pulled me closer. "Oh, of course."

I wanted to smack the gloating smirk off his face.

"And then I must figure out what to do with your neighbor. I expect I'll be seeing him soon."

Neighbor? Matt? He knew about Matt. I bit my tongue. We turned around the corner of the cabin and walked past my car, then Mary's. A second later, overgrown raspberry bushes screened us from the rest of the resort. No one would see us. We climbed the short, steep slope to the service road behind the cabin.

"It's fitting that you disappear on the same night the other bitch got her last farewells." He sounded happy. He *was* happy. He liked what he was doing. "I'm glad your friend left you for me. If he'd done his job, I wouldn't have the pleasure of your company tonight."

My neighbor. My friend. Surely, he didn't mean Matt. Who then?

My dog walked beside me, sending out a thin, worried whine I had never heard from him before.

An SUV stood behind Mary's cabin, huge and black and menacing. I nearly had a heart attack. I stumbled. Bear pressed against my leg. Devine opened the side door. He slid his arm down to my waist and tightened his grip until I couldn't move. Inside, there was a dark-colored blanket on the floor with an indistinct shape under it. He lifted the blanket. Jordy lay sprawled, limbs loose and limp, just like Travis. "See? Just what you asked for."

I yelled, "Rip him up, Bear."

My dog circled, then leaped. Devine spun and yanked me in front of him. In midair, my dog twisted away and landed beside me.

As Devine's knife slashed downward, I pushed Bear away with my foot. A long gash opened the flesh in my calf; blood ran down my leg. It didn't hurt. I didn't feel it at all. My leg belonged to someone else. My knees shook so hard I could hardly stand, and I sagged against the killer.

"Just for that, bitch, I have a gift for you." He brought his knife up and drew it lightly under my chin, all the way across my throat. It burned the way a paper cut burns. I pulled myself upright.

This man was a playground bully. In my gut, I felt certain that before he killed me, he'd make me watch Bear die, and Jordan. Not if I could help it. I pointed across the dusty, narrow road. "Good boy, sit."

Bear obeyed but prodded the ground with his forepaws and rocked side to side. He moaned, low and worried.

I gritted my teeth and pictured sticking my fingers in Devine's eyes, the way I'd heard you should, but I was trapped against his body. "Okay, big man. You've got a knife. You've drugged innocent kids. Wow. I'm impressed. What's next?"

He tossed me into the back of the SUV. I fell on top of Jordan, and Devine pushed my legs in. The door clicked shut. I struggled to my knees, holding my breath against the pain from my ribs. There was no release handle on the inside. I crawled toward the front door, but he hopped into the driver's seat and started the engine. "Let the games begin."

He sounded happy again.

Whatever happened, I would not grovel. "You won't get away with this, you piece of shit." I laced my voice with scorn. "This place is crawling with agents."

His chuckle grew into a long, low, pleasured laugh. "Your fool neighbor is on my list for tonight too, so we can't dawdle. He had his chance, you know." And then, in a perfect imitation of Bill Harlan's baritone, he said, "I've known Heather since she was a kid. Leave her alone. She can't remember a thing. She can't identify us anyway." Devine guffawed. "Idiot. The material I have to work with."

Omigod. Bill. One of them. That's why he always has money. The morning the boat ran down Ken Lagazo, he'd begged Devine to stop bludgeoning him. It was *his* voice I'd heard, but I hadn't recognized it.

And later, when I was so glad to see him, I blabbed, fool that I was, in spite of Jake's warning. Now this creep planned to murder both of us. But, please, God, not Jordy.

The SUV bounced up Sam's service road, then the tires crunched up the gravel driveway and we turned right onto smooth pavement. We were headed up-lake toward my family's cabin.

There were only two seats in the vehicle, both in the front, and only one door handle, on the driver's side. No way to get out. Blacked-out windows all around the back. No one could see me. A large metal box, like a building contractor's tool bin, occupied one side. I couldn't open it. Two big padlocks secured the lid. There was nothing I could use. I crouched on the floor beside Jordy. His breathing was slow and shallow, but regular. I put my hand on his chest and felt the slow but steady beat of his heart.

"Jordy," I said. "Wake up. Try to wake up."

"Hoping the kid will save you? You're pathetic."

"Like you're not. Picking on a boy." Shivers ran down my back. "What did you do to him?"

"Keep it up. I like a woman with spirit."

197

I used Grandma Garnet's haughtiest tone. "Well?"

"He's had some great stuff, top grade." Devine sounded pleased. "Too bad he can't enjoy it."

"You're nothing but a cheap, cheesy thug for hire."

He threw a look of pure venom at me.

"If you're such hot stuff, Devine, what are you doing in a backwater like this?"

"That's what you think, sweetheart. I'm the best. A hell of a lot of money flows through these backwater mountains, and I'm the one who keeps the pipeline open."

"Sam and Jake O'Toole and the FBI are onto you."

"Won't do you any good, baby," he crooned.

"You killed Mariella. You killed Ken Lagazo. But you didn't kill me."

"I don't do people who are sleeping. What fun would that be?"

He turned halfway around in his seat and grinned at me. "So, here's how it's going down. I hid a bomb in that fancy craft in your boathouse. You're going to take your daddy's shiny new toy out, and I'm going to blow it up, unless you find the bomb first, of course, and disarm it."

In Dad's runabout, the wheel, throttle, and gauges were in the middle, with a couple of comfy captain's chairs. Cushioned seats lined both the bow and stern, and they all had storage lockers under them. It would take forever to search each compartment, and even if I found it, how would I defuse a bomb?

"You won't have much time. You can search for the bomb, or you can jump overboard and try to swim to shore, in which case, I'll have to shoot you. As you might guess, that will make my job more difficult. I'll probably miss once or twice." He paused and glanced back, as if to read my expression. "Your way or my way, you're going to be fully aware of what's happening and who's doing it to you, baby."

I couldn't speak. I shook from head to toe. But I would not give him the satisfaction of breaking down.

"The best part is, I'll get to see how fond you are of that kid. You'll have a better chance if you swim, see, and leave him to get blown up in the boat. If you drag him along, I'll shoot him first." He looked back at me again with a smug, supercilious smile. "You might as well get used to the idea. He's gone. Poof!" He cackled as if that was the funniest line ever.

The psychopath in the driver's seat was about to have an orgasm up there, just thinking about killing Jordan, then me and my fool neighbor.

Bear was my only hope. Surely, he would have followed the SUV. He'd run as he did when I jogged in the mornings, a black shadow in the trees and brush beside the road. Four and a half miles. Nearly fifteen minutes.

I should have figured it out. Bill, Tom's old fishing buddy, knew better than anyone how deep and cold our cove is and that none of us were likely to be there. Why had he invited me to go out in his boat a few minutes ago? Was he in on this plan to blow me up? I took a long breath and held it in, trying to steady myself.

My captor whistled. He drove slowly. I got the sick feeling that he wanted to draw it out, enjoy it a little while longer. Run, Bear. My only hope. Run. Run. Run.

We bumped off the road into the familiar driveway and drove right into the carport, where we were hidden from passersby on the road. I had no more time. I had to think of a way to keep Jordy alive. If he died, it would be my fault.

Devine walked around and pulled the side door open. "Ladies first." Holding out his hand, he grinned. "Allow me." Again, the horrible parody of a date. When I didn't take his hand, he gripped my arm.

"Keep your filthy hands to yourself, dirt bag." As I stepped onto the gravel, I tried to shake him off.

"My pleasure." He turned and bent over to lift Jordan.

I scooped up a handful of gravel and flung it at him as hard as I could. It was stupid. Pain ripped through my ribs, and the pebbles merely bounced off his back; I didn't care. I snatched more. He pivoted to face me, and I peppered Jordan with my pebbles.

He pulled out a revolver. "Go ahead. One more tantrum and he gets it." He tucked the long, silenced barrel into the boy's side, at heart level. The light would go out of those dancing hazel eyes forever, and no one would even hear. All the fight drained out of me.

With a jerk of his chin, Devine indicated I was to lead the way around the cabin. "It's time for our adventure on the water. I'm looking forward to it. And I'm sure you are, too."

I stumbled along the path beside the cabin and up onto the deck, wishing I dared yell for help, doubting that my voice would carry far enough, afraid there was no one to hear, afraid yelling would hasten our deaths.

The bastard held Jordy with just one arm and showed no sign of the effort it took to carry him. I skirted the hot tub and pointed to the spot where I liked to sleep, in front of the sliding door. "Put him down." I crossed my arms and glared.

"I am sick of your mouth." He swung the pistol. It cracked against the side of my head. I staggered and fell against the table behind me. Dazed, I stared at the blood dripping down the front of Mary's linen dress.

"Now, isn't that too bad?" I didn't see him exchange the gun for his knife, but with a second sweep of his hand, he sliced the knife tip downward from the neckline, opening the pale blue fabric, exposing my rib belt and bare breasts. He grabbed the back of the dress and yanked it down until, except for the rib support, I was bare from my waist up. The slit edges pinned my arms to my sides. "That looks quite fetching." He leered at me.

"May you roast in hell." My face hurt so much that I could hardly speak, but I did my best to sound cool and contemptuous. I shrugged the dress back up onto my shoulders. "Kill me if you want to. Right here. I'm not going to play your game with the boat."

"The kid's first." Slowly, he drew the tip of his knife around Jordan's neck, slicing a delicate red gash, like mine. He watched my face, smiling, then held the knife tip against Jordy's shoulder blade. "I can kill him a bit at a time if you wish."

"Stop! I'll go to the dock."

If this pervert killed her son, he will have killed Mary, too. My ears rang from the blow to my head. Dizzy, slobbering, bleeding onto Mary's ruined dress, I staggered down the long flight of stairs to the lake.

"See how much nicer it is when you cooperate?"

I pulled my back up straight. Bear would cut through Cowans' yard and follow the path between our two cabins. If the Cowans had arrived a little early, they'd see him. They'd think it odd. They'd come over.

Then they'd call Jake.

Somehow, I made it to the bottom and plodded along the dock to the boathouse, keeping each step straight and firm.

"The fun is about to begin."

Dad's boat rested quietly in the gloom of the boathouse. Sunset light bounced off the water and shimmered on polished sides. I don't know why, but suddenly I felt calm. "So, tell me, is your little bomb set to go off at a certain time?"

"Now that would be pretty dumb, wouldn't it? And it wouldn't be much fun. A remote detonator is a far superior choice." He smirked, as if applauding his own brilliance. "Spontaneity is good." He leaned forward and dumped Jordan into the boat. Jordy's legs hit first, then his body flopped down and his head whip-lashed back, banged hard on the floor. He lay, not moving, between the captain's chairs in the middle and the padded seats in the stern.

"You maggot-infested, dickless wonder. You won't get away with this. Jake is on his way."

He grabbed a handful of my hair and jerked my head back. "I don't know any Jakes. Is he your lover? Does he kiss you like this?" He forced his tongue into my mouth. I tried to bite it, but my head was back so far I couldn't close my jaws. I tried to kick him but missed.

He shoved the dress open and rubbed my bare breasts with the barrel of his gun, scraping harshly over the nipples. "I just wonder if you wouldn't enjoy my barrel down here." The hard metal drifted down over my belly, down one thigh, and then up again. All the while he watched my face. "If we had time, I'd show you a real good time."

I clamped my teeth into his shoulder. He jerked back. I grabbed his balls and twisted with every ounce of strength I had. He doubled over.

I jumped into the boat and started the engine. I threw the lines off, jammed it into gear, and backed out as fast as I could. By the time I was out of the boathouse, he had straightened up again to his full height. He pointed the gun at me. "Bitch."

As I spun the wheel and turned into the cove, a bullet smashed the windscreen on my left. I hit the throttle. The stern sank down in the water, and we took off. I squatted low in front of the captain's chair and zigzagged, one hand gripping the bottom of the wheel. Another bullet shattered the glass on my right.

Maybe we were going to be blown to smithereens, but that would be better than the feel of Devine's hands on my body. I headed toward a narrow point that jutted out into the cove and marked the line between Cowans' property and ours. The breeze had kicked up a light chop. If I could get Jordan out of the boat, I had a chance. In the water, the long, slanting rays of light bouncing off the waves would make it difficult to for Devine to see. But first, I had to get far enough away.

"Jordy," I yelled, "Jordy. Wake up. Wake up."

A boat just like Dad's turned from the lake into the cove, speeding toward me. Bill.

I veered away from him, toward shore, then turned the engine off to stop the propeller. I grabbed Jordy under the armpits and tried to lift him. Mary's dress slid down off my shoulders. I jerked it off and tossed it on the floor.

I'll never know how I did it, but I got Jordy all the way up onto the seat, then lifted his legs and feet over the edge of the boat. I was ready to push him into the water when Bill came alongside. In a moment, he was there, in my boat. He scooped the boy up in his arms and stepped back into his own boat. "Come on," he yelled. "He's going to blow you up."

I grabbed his hand and leaped. His arms flew wide and his body arched, then jerked again and again. He dropped Jordan and, in slow motion, collapsed on top of him. I fell to my knees beside them.

I heard a loud whoosh, and a scorching blast slammed me flat. For several moments, I couldn't see. I couldn't move. Then, as my mind cleared, I got to hands and knees and peered over the side. Dad's boat was gone. Bill's boat was running at an idle and we were circling back toward the cabin, getting close to our dock—and the assassin. I couldn't see Jordy except for his copper colored hair and one arm under Bill's legs.

Staying low, I crawled over the motionless Bill. He didn't make a sound. His back was a mass of raw flesh and shredded fabric, slippery with blood. I gagged. I stopped for a moment and held my breath, then made it to the helm. I gripped the wheel and raised my head far enough to look through the bottom of the windscreen. We were scary close.

In the fading light, Devine stood on the dock, waiting. I opened the throttle and spun the wheel hard left, turning away. The gauges shattered right in front of me. I zigzagged. Right. Left. Right. Bullets whizzed past me and tore into the boat. The motor sputtered, coughed, slowed. Keeping just one hand on the wheel, I crouched as low as I could and looked back over the open stern.

Behind Devine and above him on the rocks, a black

shape—Bear—silent—bunched for a leap. My dog launched himself, forepaws extended. He came down on Devine's shoulders with his full weight and bulk. The man's arms flew up and he went down flat on the dock with my dog on top of him. The pistol arched high in the air and splashed into the water.

I turned back toward shore. "Good boy!" I shouted. "Rip him up!" I stood at the helm and headed in to pick up my dog.

Devine somehow got Bear off his back and rolled to his feet. I caught the glint of steel in his hand. He slashed at Bear. My dog faltered. He limped. But he clamped his jaws onto the killer's arm and gave it a sharp twist. With a yowl of pain, the man dropped the knife.

Fierce pride surged through my heart. "Rip him up, Bear. Get him."

Devine's arm dangled at his side. "Bitch," he snarled. It was the last word he ever spoke. The whine of high-powered rifles rent the air. He crumpled onto the dock.

A small, cold hand grasped my ankle. Jordy struggled out from under Bill. "Oh, man, what's happening? Geez, Heather, where's your clothes?"

The motor was barely running. I prayed for it to keep going. Bear collapsed to his knees, and then tried to push himself back up. "I'm coming," I shouted. He struggled to stand on all fours. Blood poured down the white swatch on his chest.

I banged the boat against the dock. "Come here, baby. Come in the boat." I held out my arms and he tumbled in. I rolled him over and found the wound, a gash in his fur between his chest wall and shoulder. I pulled the edges together and clamped them with my fist. Resting one paw on my arm, he whimpered but let me do it.

"Oh, man, what happened?" Jordy pulled off his T-shirt, wadded it up, and handed it to me. "Holy cow, this is amazing."

I heard feet running on the dock. I heard Matt call my name. I didn't even look up. I couldn't move. Not with my best friend's life draining through my fingers.

Chapter Twenty

I struggled to hold the edges of Bear's wound together and put pressure on it, but with each beat of his heart, more blood pumped out. My own heart beat wildly. I screamed for help, but the boat had drifted away from the dock. Jordy found a line and threw it, but he had little of his usual strength, and the line splashed into the water.

Seconds later, Matt climbed up over the transom. He leaned over me for a moment, dripping icy water. "You're doing the right thing." He flipped up seat cushions until he found a flannel shirt. He pulled a knife out of his pocket and shredded the shirt into long strips. "Jordan, start rolling these up." He folded Jordy's T-shirt into a pad. "If we can press this against the wound, then wrap these strips around him, maybe we can stop the bleeding. Sound okay, Heather?"

I nodded.

Matt knelt in front of me. "Keep the edges clamped together and press Jordy's shirt down. Hold it as tight as you can." He rolled a strip around Bear and pulled it tight. Bear's whimpers hurt my heart. I held his head on my lap. I couldn't speak. Matt wound another strip around and knotted it firmly. It was already soaked with blood.

I was vaguely aware that an inflatable police boat had pulled up beside us. It pushed us back to the dock.

Suddenly Jake was there. "Need a couple of medics over here," he yelled. He grabbed the lines and tied us to a cleat. "Heather. Jordan. Thank God." He got in and knelt beside Matt. "And Bear." He lifted Bear a bit to make it easier for Matt to wind the flannel around his chest. I felt his eyes on me. "Thank God."

A medic climbed in, crouched beside Bill, and jostled for space to check his pulse, then shouted for help. Another guy arrived and together with Jake, they lifted Bill to the dock and carried him to a stretcher.

The sheriff came back and squatted beside the boat. He put his hand on Jordy's head. "You okay, son?"

"Yeah. But Bear isn't."

"Come on, then, let's get you out of there." While Jake steadied the boat, Jordan stood and started to climb out, but wobbled and toppled backward.

"Jordy!" I screeched.

Jake grabbed him and pulled him up. He crumpled onto the dock. Jake put an arm around him and helped him sit up, then sat beside him. The boy leaned against the sheriff's chest.

Sirens shrieked up above at the cabin. Bright lights flashed in the water. Feet pounded down the stairs. A medic squatted beside Jordy and shone a flashlight in his eyes. "No. No." Jordy closed his eyes and shook his head. "Help Bear." He waved the medic away. "Please. I'm okay. Help Bear. He's bleeding bad."

When the medic hesitated, Jordy sat up straight. "You better not let Bear die."

The man turned and peered down at my dog. "Has he lost a lot of blood?"

"A lot." Matt tied the last length of flannel in a snug knot and pressed both hands down on mine, over the wound. "We can't stop it."

The medic got in. He opened his bag and selected a razor. "Hold his leg still for me." Matt held Bear's leg. A patch of fur fell neatly away, leaving his leg white and soft and vulnerable. An instant later, a needle slid under the skin and the medic taped a tube down. He climbed out. "Be right back."

Bear's heart beat rapidly. His pulse felt weak and thready under my fingers. His eyes were closed and his head lolled to the side. Matt and I pressed down hard.

More men appeared. They marched around, issuing orders. Jake helped Jordan to his feet and lifted him onto a stretcher. A man in a uniform put a blanket over him and strapped him in, then started pushing him toward the stairs.

My heart nearly stopped. "Where are you taking Jordan?"

Matt was talking to me, telling me not to worry.

The man kept pushing the stretcher away.

Still holding Bear, I tried to get to my feet. "Stop! You can't take him away."

Jake got into the boat with us. He put his hands on my shoulders. "It's okay, Heather. He needs to go. Mary will meet him at the hospital. She and Travis are there now."

I slumped back into the seat and hugged my dog hard. Tears ran down my face and I didn't know why.

The medic returned. "Let's get this IV started." He handed a bag of fluid to Jake and attached a line to the tube he had taped to my dog's leg. When the IV started to flow, he wrapped a wide white bandage around it all and taped it all to a padded board. "That will fix you up, old fella."

If only he was right.

He smiled at me. "You're next."

I held up my hand, palm out. "I need to get Bear to the vet."

"You have some injuries that need care."

"No."

He took my hand, put a couple of fingers on my pulse, and peered into my eyes. "I don't think you realize how badly you're hurt. Let me help you."

I pulled away. "It doesn't matter."

"I have to be clear about this." His tone was even, soft. "Are you refusing treatment?"

My jaw throbbed. My back felt as if the skin had been scraped off. The pain in my ribs was sharper than ever. None of it mattered. "I am. I'm fine."

Matt took my chin in his hand and made me look at him. "Heather, you are not fine. You need help."

I glared at him. "*I said no*." I shook his hand off. "I need to take care of Bear."

"Give it up," Jake said. "You might as well do what she wants."

Matt frowned.

Jake put a foot up onto the dock. "Sam can take you two and Bear in his boat. He's already called the vet and asked him to meet you at the wharf. Then you can get Heather to the hospital."

"Sounds like you're sure about that," Matt said. He scowled at me, waited a couple of moments, and when I didn't budge, he pressed his lips into a thin line. "Okay. Fine," he said. "I don't like it, but let's go. I'll carry Bear." Matt got his arms under my dog. He grunted as he straightened up and climbed out of the boat. Holding the IV bag up high, Jake put an arm around me and helped me out. My knees wobbled. I could hardly walk.

Four men were starting up the stairs, carrying Bill on his stretcher. Soon the dock would be empty again. Except for one dead man lying under a blanket, one arm trailing in the water. We had to step over him. I held onto Jake's arm and fixed my gaze on Matt's back.

At some point, Sam had motored in. There wasn't room for his boat to tie up so he'd backed the stern in behind Bill's boat. "I have to stay here," Jake said as he grabbed the handrail on Sam's stern and pulled it closer.

Once the boat was secured, Jake looked down at me, his expression grave. "If I'd arrested Bill when I wanted to, it's unlikely that we would have caught Devine. As it is, he's not going to cause any more trouble. That's the good news." He shook his head. "The bad news is that when I agreed to wait, I promised to protect you. We all did. But we failed you. *I* failed you, and I am humbly, deeply sorry."

He helped me onto Sam's boat and handed me Bear's IV bag. "I promise you'll be safe tonight, and from now on." To Matt, he said, "See that you get her to the hospital."

Matt turned, still cradling Bear. He looked at me with a funny smile on his face. "*I'm* going to get her to go? Why don't *you* have that discussion with her?"

But Jake just stepped back and watched as we motored away.

It hurt me to see defeat written on his face.

The vet met us at the wharf in town, ready to transport Bear. Matt and I went along. Sam returned to the resort to make sure Mary's cabin, now a crime scene, had been secured.

The animal hospital was small, but spotless and white. The lights were on, and an assistant was setting up the operating room when we got there. I was allowed to stay with Bear until the anesthetic took effect, and then I had to go to the waiting room, where Matt stood, looking out the window into the darkness, talking on his phone.

He kept his voice low, but clearly, he was angry. His tone had a bite in it. "Got it. Got it." He listened for several seconds, then said, "Then tell them this. They need to find out how Devine got from there to here without anyone knowing." He stomped to the door. "I need some air."

He flung it open, stomped outside, and stood on the steps, still talking into the phone, yelling was more like it. Finally, he turned around and came back in, scowling. "That was the agent in the FBI office in Paris. He's talking to Interpol. They say the local police have been watching Devine, and as far as anyone over there knows, he's still at a compound owned by a couple of drug lords near Nice. What a bunch of shit! Shit! Shit! Shit!"

He jammed his phone into a pocket and crossed his arms on his chest. "Sorry. I'm spouting off. But they damn sure better find a reason." He clamped his mouth shut and refused to say more.

Sam Fitzpatrick arrived in his pickup. He brought cookies, sandwiches, and a thermos of coffee packed in a wicker basket, and a folded set of sweats. "Penny's first aid kit," he said as he set the basket on a chair. "Funny thing is, it works." Straightening, he looked at me and flinched. Then he put his hand on my shoulder. "Is there anything I can do for you?"

I shook my head. My mouth hurt too much to talk.

"Jake's a wuss," Matt said. "He couldn't talk her into going to the hospital, so he told me to do it. You can see how successful I was." He kicked the leg of a chair. "How successful I am all around."

"Well then," Sam replied, "I guess that's why he called Alicia Mendosa."

The smell of Penny's tuna sandwiches nauseated me. I resumed my pacing between the waiting room and the closed door of the surgery. I'd swallowed a couple ibuprofen while on Sam's boat but my head still throbbed. The skin on my back felt stretched tight and hot. My ribs ached like hell. I had to keep moving, even though I could barely make my feet shuffle forward. Everything hurt too much to sit still. I nearly caved in and said I'd go to the hospital, but just then headlights shone in the window. A car door closed and Alicia came into the clinic. She stopped abruptly and dropped her black bag when she saw me. Behind me, Matt rested a hand lightly on the small of my back.

For a moment, Alicia just stood there, eyes wide. Her mouth opened and closed. Then her gaze swept from my head down to my toes, and back up again. I looked down. Someone had put a man's white shirt on me. It had been soaked with blood, which had dried in dark red-brown splotches. My arms and legs were streaked with the same color. Under my fingernails, the blood had turned black. I stared at them as Alicia came and turned me gently around. She put a cool hand up and lightly touched my scalp. "The sheriff asked me to come over. I can see why."

At that moment, Sam came back from his explorations. "I found a bathroom with a shower behind the office, and some clean towels." He tipped his head in the direction he'd come from. "I left the light on."

"Excellent." She herded me toward the light. "First, let's get some medication in you." She opened a bottle of water and gave me a handful of pills. I swallowed them in one big gulp.

Then she said, "I'll help you clean up." She turned on the shower and helped me ease the shirt off.

I sat on a little plastic stool and scrubbed my arms and legs with soap that smelled like the corridor in the hospital. Alicia's pills made me dizzy, but the cool water felt good on my back. As the blood came off and sluiced away down the drain, I wondered whether some of it was Bill's. I scrubbed harder. I didn't want his blood on me. It felt intrusive and terrible.

Finally, I put my hands up and touched my head. I had no hair. My scalp felt scorched, like my back, as if I had a third-degree sunburn. At first, I thought I was totally bald, but then I found a fringe of hair just above my forehead. Alicia's pills made me giggle.

Very gently, she patted my back dry and then sprayed my head and back with what she called an analgesic mist. It felt cool and sticky. She cut a strip of clear, shiny dressing and pressed it over the thin red line on my throat. "That will feel better now, and it'll heal ten times faster."

She wrapped a wide Ace bandage snugly around my ribs and massaged a soothing lotion into my hands, arms, and legs. She stood by, hands out, ready to grab me if I lost my balance, as I got into Penny's sweats. Then she let me look in the mirror.

One side of my face, where Devine hit me with the pistol, had ballooned to the size of a small eggplant. My eye had half disappeared beneath the swelling. Alicia's pills made me think it didn't matter, that maybe that wasn't even me. I traced the knife wound on my neck with a fingertip. I felt as if I was watching from far away. But that was me in the mirror, all right. Devine had done that to me.

"He had a lot of skill with that knife," I said in words beginning to slur. "He cut Jordan the same way. I think I was supposed to be impressed."

"Do you want to talk about what happened?"

I shook my head.

"Tomorrow, or anytime, if you change your mind, just let me know."

I stared at my hair. It stood up above my forehead like a tiara, a frizzled ruff about an inch long. I put my fingers up to feel the brittle, singed ends. "Maybe I should dye this purple to match my face."

Alicia smiled. "You are amazing."

"No." I shook my head. "I promised God that if Jordy survived, I would never again complain about anything." My lips quivered and tears started down my cheeks. "And now, all I care about is Bear. If my dog lives through this, I'll be the luckiest person alive."

"I see." She nodded. "Come lie on the couch in the office and let me check you over." She led the way into a cramped but tidy room. Besides a heavy oak desk, there was a huge oak file cabinet and a big black leather sofa. Along one wall, there was a mini kitchen with a bar sink, a little refrigerator, a coffee maker, and a microwave.

Alicia helped me lie down on my side, lifting my feet and sliding my legs onto the cushions. She looked at my mouth inside and out, and then did all the usual doctor things, including a few painful pokes and prods. At last, she put her stethoscope in her black bag, pulled up a chair, and sat beside me. "It would be a good idea to go to the hospital tonight. I could give you stronger medication, and you'd be able to sleep."

I put my hand up, palm facing her. "I can't. I wouldn't sleep at all. I hate the hospital."

"I thought you might say that." She rummaged in her bag and brought out a pill bottle, which she put in my hand, and a card. "You can take two of these, every three or four hours. In small doses, for a short period of time, they shouldn't harm your liver, but you need to come and see me tomorrow. In the meantime, my home phone and my cell numbers are on there. Phone me if you change your mind or if need me for anything, night or day, okay?"

After she left, Sam and Matt came into the room. They insisted that I rest. "Try to sleep," they said. They meant it kindly, but as soon as I fell asleep, vivid images appeared.

Devine holding the pistol to Jordy's heart, Devine forcing his tongue into my mouth, Bill falling and dropping Jordy, Devine slicing my throat; each time, I jerked awake again, my eyes wide, my heart pounding, and my breath coming in gasps. Sam and Matt chatted quietly. Clearly, Sam knew or had guessed pretty much the whole story. They ate tuna sandwiches and chocolate chip cookies and drank coffee and waited.

At last the surgery door opened, and the vet's footsteps came briskly toward us. Matt helped me up, and we flocked to meet him. I held my breath until he pulled his mask off and smiled. "Glad you warmed my couch up, young lady. I think Bear will be fine, but I'm going to stay here tonight."

I couldn't speak. Tears gushed; my breathing came in short, rolling grunts. I sounded like an old goat and didn't much care.

Matt kept one arm around me in support, held my hand with his free one. Sam stepped forward. "That's excellent news. We'll be at my place. You'll call, won't you, if anything happens?"

"Certainly, but I don't expect any problems." The vet peered at me over the top of his bifocals. He looked like my dad, which made me cry all the harder. His forehead wrinkled in concern. He offered a box of tissues and patted my shoulder. "Try not to worry. Bear is young and strong, and I'll take good care of him." He went to his desk and gave me a card. "My phone number."

Sam picked up a pen. "I'll write mine down. She'll be with me."

Matt pulled a card out of his wallet. "Or with me."

By the time we got into Sam's truck, the three of us had coalesced into a single entity with one purpose: to get back to the resort. It was two o'clock in the morning when Sam pulled in beside his house. Matt helped me down out of the truck. We crossed the patio and went into the kitchen. The light over the sink shone down and bounced off the stainless steel, giving an other-worldly glow to the room.

Mary and Penny burst in from the living room, turned on an overhead light, and stopped. Penny put her hand to her mouth. "Oh, honey."

Mary rushed at me, tears shining in her eyes. Without speaking, she took both of my hands. "I'm glad they didn't keep you in the hospital."

Sam said, "Hah. She wouldn't go near it. The doc had to come to her."

"I couldn't go there." The very idea still made me stiffen with fear. "They'd sedate me so I'd sleep, but when I close my eyes, it starts all over again and it's worse. Besides, I have to stay awake for Bear."

Mary and Penny both stared at me. After a moment, Penny said, "You are absolutely right. You belong here with us."

"I'm fine, really."

Penny shook her head. "No, you are not, but I know you will be, and Bear will be, too."

Mary started to cry again. "He has to be okay."

Penny turned Mary around and nudged her toward the door. "He will be. Why don't you all go into the living room? I'll make us something to eat."

Matt ran a hand down the front of his shirt. "I must look pretty disgusting." Although it had once been white, the shirt was completely red-brown. Large splotches of dried blood stained his khaki shorts. "I'll run upstairs and take a shower. Be right back."

Sam and I followed Mary into the spacious living room. On the far wall, a fire burned in the huge fieldstone fireplace. On either side, sofas faced each other. One of them had been opened up to make a bed. The boys, faces shining in the soft light, lay side by side, sleeping. The fire crackled and spit. Firelight danced across the windows and reflected back into the room, making it feel safe and warm.

As I gazed at Jordan, then Travis, then Jordan again, the burning pain on my back, the throbbing in my jaw, and the ache in my ribs faded. No words could ever express my gratitude. All I could say was, "I'm so glad to see them." They looked just as normal as ever, except Jordy's forehead sported a giant bruise on one side and he had a shiny dressing like mine on his neck. "Jordy slept through most of it. Are they okay?"

"By morning, they'll be completely fine, even Jordan." Mary bent over and rearranged the blanket over his shoulder. "Thanks to you, Heather."

"Thanks to me?" I croaked. I could hardly form the words. "Thanks to me, he got in trouble to start with."

Mary perched on the sofa-bed, right next to her son. "It wasn't your fault."

My knees wouldn't hold me any longer. I sank down on the other side, beside Travis, and drew in a deep breath. "It *was* my fault. If I'd stayed in Seattle, acted like an adult, told Alex how I felt about him, and set some limits on the relationship, none of this would have happened."

Sam poked at the fire. "Now, where did that bit of wisdom come from?" He added another log, then sat on the other sofa and leaned forward, elbows on knees, blue eyes serious, an earnest expression on his weathered face. "Tonight wouldn't have happened, but a man was killed up at your place and if you hadn't been there, no one would have been the wiser. We wouldn't have had a clue about where he was or what had happened to him."

"Exactly," Mary said. "And most likely, Bill would have gotten away with murder, and we would all be thinking what a great guy he is because he sponsors the high school soccer team."

Sam mimicked Jake's habit of scuffing his fingertips through his hair. It made thick, gingery tufts stick out above his ears. "And Mariella? I suppose we might have found her body eventually, and maybe we would have figured out she'd been murdered. We would have blamed Ken Lagazo, since his wallet was in the car. We'd have believed that he escaped but got disoriented and drowned. Everybody would have said, 'Aha! That's what happened to him.'" Sam sent me a slow, reluctant grin. "We'd have gotten it completely wrong, and the bad guys would have won."

A weight lifted off my heart. I could breathe again.

Sam said, "All of us would be a good deal happier right now, I suppose, if we didn't know what actually happened."

"Does anyone know how Devine got to the boys?" I had to know.

"We were all over here. That made it easy for him," Sam said. "It probably took less than five minutes."

Matt came in from the kitchen, carrying a plate of muffins. "Sixty seconds, max. A couple of injections, and the kids were out." He tripped over the edge of the carpet and muffins flew off the plate. Sam helped him pick them up, and they stuck them on the coffee table.

Matt grabbed one and bit into it. "Five second rule." He had pulled his wet hair back in a pony-tail and put on a pair of black jeans, taut across lean hips, and a starched white shirt with the sleeves rolled back. Did that mean his job was finished, that he didn't need his carefree-guy-on-vacation disguise anymore? My heart felt a little pang. I was sort of fond of the baggy shorts and T-shirt with the faded rock stars on the front.

Mary stood up and stretched her back. "Who was he, Matt?"

"You mean Devine?"

"Yes." She bent down and smoothed a hand over Jordy's forehead.

Matt leaned against the mantel. "Devore David Devine, a fixer for a couple of drug lords in South America. The DEA was getting close to understanding their distribution ring, and sent Ken Lagazo to verify that Bill was laundering money for them. Either Bill thought Ken was trying to horn in on his piece of the action and squealed, or someone broke Ken's cover, and the drug bosses sent Devine to get rid of him."

Mary said, "Heather couldn't identify him, so how did you know who it was?"

"Simone Rideau saw him on the mail boat the day of Ken's murder," Matt said.

"Aha! So she *did* see him," Mary said. "She came over in the middle of the hail storm to ask if we thought she should tell Jake about a man who got on board at the fire lookout station. He didn't have a backpack or even a daypack, and she thought that was strange."

"Right. She picked him out of a photo lineup without hesitation. Why he offed Ken with help from an amateur like Bill Harlan I don't know. He probably had orders to make sure Harlan was in too deep to talk."

Mary paced back and forth in front of the fire. "Why did they kill Mariella?"

"My guess is that she was a risk simply because she'd been with Ken, and since Devine needed to dispose of that car, he wrapped it all up in one tidy package. Besides, I think he enjoyed killing." Matt gazed at me, looking puzzled. "What I don't understand is why he left you down in that ravine without making sure you were gone."

"Jake thinks he decided she couldn't possibly

survive," Sam said. "That way, Ken was dead. Mariella couldn't talk. Bill's mouth was sealed. The only witness was the victim of a hit and run. Job done."

Finally, I spoke up. "He told me that since I wasn't awake, it wouldn't have been fun."

Matt shuddered. "I can believe that. He had antisocial tendencies similar to many serial killers. As crazy as it is, that may be what kept you alive." He shook his head. "Whichever way it went down, he headed off to the French Riviera where his bosses maintain a big compound for R and R."

Mary frowned. "How did he get back here undetected?"

Matt looked grim. "When we learned he was in France, one of our agents in Paris worked with Interpol and the local police to set up cameras to watch the compound. Tonight, when I told him Devine was here, the agent got in touch with the police. They discovered that the system has been looping random videos of him lounging around the compound for the last four days, making it look as if he was still there. You can bet some tails are in a wringer over the security of the surveillance software."

Penny came in from the kitchen with a big pot of tea. "Sam! What on earth is wrong with you? Bring the recliner close to the fire. Heather, I can't believe these guys aren't taking better care of you." Sam dragged the chair over, and Penny helped me into it, propped up on my side so there was no weight on my back, still scolding. "Honestly, Sam, a person would think you lived in a barn."

Matt sent him a sympathetic grin, then continued, "At the moment, we have to move quickly, before the gang hears about Devine and disappears. It's huge, and it's been pulling in millions every month, but right now, multiple arrests are going on in various parts of the country. By morning, the entire ring will be rounded up and arrested. We weren't quite ready, so a few may escape, but thanks to Ken and his excellent work, they are out of business."

"Partly because of Heather," Mary said.

"With a lot of thanks to Heather." Matt smiled half a smile at me. "My hat is off to you. You did something no officer of the law has been able to do. You outsmarted a devious, dangerous assassin."

"With help from Bear," I said.

Matt nodded. "We owe that dog a lot."

I had to hold my breath for a moment so I wouldn't cry. "You and Jake got there just in time." I tried to sound nonchalant, but my voice quavered. "How did you know where to find me?"

"Charlie, of all people," Sam said. "Believe it or not, we owe that to him. He paid for Mariella's burial, by the way, and has already ordered a headstone. But that's beside the point. Got any more of those muffins, hon? Jake should be coming along any minute."

"Yes, and they'll keep better in the kitchen until he does." Penny patted her husband's midriff. "Finish the story."

"Right." Sam nodded. "Charlie's an ornery fart. Jake can't abide the sight of him, with good reason. He's no saint, but he's no dummy. He saw Bear charging up to the road after a big SUV with blacked-out windows, and he thought that was strange, so he fired up his bike and chased after it.

"In the meantime, your tracer went silent, so Matt

ran over to Mary's cabin and found Travis. We were searching the resort when Charlie came roaring back. Matt and Jake tore up to your folks' cabin, and I took my boat up in case the perp planned to slip away on the water."

I felt as if a spring had been wound up tight inside me. I started jabbering. "I never thought I'd thank Charlie for anything. I was sure he killed Mariella and tried to kill me, too. I was wrong. I owe him an apology. I owe him my life, and Bear's, and … and … Jordy's. Even Jordy's."

Mary sniffed and brushed away a tear. "What's with Bill? He has a lovely little family. Julie's a sweetheart."

Sam said, "My guess is that he found an easy way to make a lot of money."

Footsteps sounded on the kitchen floor. Jake came into the living room and peered around at us. I'd never seen him look so tired.

Penny jumped up. "Poor old Jake. I'll get you some muffins."

A grin lit his face. "I'll take one in a bit, but right now, the best aurora borealis I've seen in years is going on out there." He hitched his thumb back over his shoulder. "You all need to come and see it."

Mary dashed to the window and peered out. "Oh, wow. He's right. Hurry before it fades away. Wake the boys up."

Sam and Jake led the way, Matt and I followed, Mary and Penny came in the rear, each holding a blanket around a groggy boy. Jordy slurred his words, but that didn't stop him. "Oh, man, you should have seen it, Trav. I'm, like, lying in the bottom of the boat with this big weight on top of me, and Heather's roaring around with no hair and no clothes on. Then Bear fought the guy that tried to kill Heather, and the guy stabbed Bear in the heart. Man, it was the most amazing day I've ever had so far."

"All that happened to me," Travis said, "was I got sick to my stomach."

We stood in a cluster on the lawn, where hours before we'd held the service for Mariella, and looked up. From a point far away in the universe, so high above as to be unfathomable, vivid pinks and greens and lavenders radiated out and down, moving like softly swaying curtains, luminous and totally awesome. The water shimmered so brightly that we seemed to be immersed in dancing, dazzling color. It faded and brightened, glowed stronger here, then there; changed as soon as someone remarked on it. Standing there together, we talked about Mariella in hushed voices. It felt like the right way to say goodbye to her. And then we gave thanks for our own safety.

"It's an omen," Mary said at last, and we all agreed, although no one ever quite knew what the things Mary declared to be omens meant.

As the northern lights died away and the Milky Way resumed its reign, I felt a small, warm hand patting my arm and looked down to see Jordan standing beside me. "A good omen," he said, "for Bear."

Chapter Twenty-One

The aurora borealis had faded and disappeared. Stars glittered out of a measureless black sky. The chilly night breeze raised goose bumps on our arms and ruffled our hair, and still we lingered on the lawn, looking up. I think we were all feeling stunned by the immenseness—and the awesome power and grace of the universe. Matt stood behind me, close enough to shelter me from the breeze. I felt his warmth on my back.

"Einstein said the universe is a friendly place," he said. "And on the whole, I think he's right." The terror of the last few hours seemed to diminish a little. My heartbeat became slow and steady, and my breath flowed more easily.

Mary prodded the boys back across the patio and everyone followed. We trooped through the kitchen, still smelling of the cinnamon in Penny's muffins, and into the softly lighted living room. I shivered as I encountered the warmth of the fire again. Sam poked it with the tongs, and sparks streamed up the flue. He put another log on. I settled into the recliner and curled up sideways to keep the pressure off my back.

Yawning, Jake stretched his long arms overhead. "I'm going to head on home, but first, a couple of things." He leaned against the mantel. "Matt, join in if you want to add something." The men exchanged a glance, and as Matt nodded, I felt a current of respect flow between them. "Here's the deal. Mary, your cabin is now a crime scene, so no one goes in until I say so. Heather, same with yours. We have a man posted at each place just in case. Tonight, you're all better off together anyway, so stay here in Sam's house."

"I'm going to sleep right here on the other sofa." Mary stroked Jordan's hair back from his forehead. Both boys were already asleep again.

Penny said, "There's plenty of room for you, too, Heather."

"Fine." Jake pressed his lips together. "Here's the next thing: until I tell you it's okay, none of what you've heard, and none of what happened tonight goes outside this room. Clear?" He looked at each of us and in turn, we nodded. "Matt assures me that by morning, the arrests will be completed, but there are other factors."

Matt looked at his watch. "If all goes well, by seven, Eastern Daylight Time."

"What about the body in the orchard, the one Sam found when the snow melted?" Mary asked. "Is there a correlation?"

Matt said, "It was the body in the orchard that led the DEA to Bill, the first solid clue that he was involved. The money, which Bill laundered, arrived by courier, and this particular courier got greedy. It took a while to figure out who he was and why he was here because there was nothing on his body to identify him, and he had no fingerprints."

Mary's eyes opened wide. "No fingerprints?"

"No hands, therefore, no fingerprints."

Collectively, the rest of us gasped. Matt looked as

if he was thinking. "Until all the arrests are made, I'd better shut up. But I don't think Bill meant to get in as deep as he did."

Jake said, "I know for a fact he was supposed to finish Heather off. When he came to see her in the hospital, he had enough morphine to stop the hearts of several people."

"Seriously?" Penny, Mary, and I chorused.

"Yup," Jake answered. "Remember, Heather? Orlando made him empty his pockets, and found what Bill claimed was an insulin pen. I suppose he expected he'd find you alone. As it was, if he'd made any attempt to administer it, Orlando would have arrested his butt. Of course, he didn't, and when he failed to harm you, he signed his death warrant." Jake frowned. "I should have wised up sooner. Right away, I should have taken you to town and sat on you. I should never have left you alone, especially knowing you'd told Bill."

Mary shook her head. "But he's been a pillar of the community. This will come as a huge shock to Julie. And now he may die."

Jake heaved out a sigh. "That's about it."

That moment when I took Bill's hand and leaped into his boat flashed into my mind. "He tried to redeem himself." I saw him fall, as vividly as if it were happening again. "I won't be able to sleep tonight. I can't even think about closing my eyes."

Matt came and stood beside the recliner. "I have some ghosts of my own to deal with tonight." He held out his hand to help me up. "What if we go down to my boat and look at the stars for a while?"

While Sam opened the second sofa bed and Penny

gathered mugs, Jake, Matt, and I walked outside. I said goodnight to Jake on the patio. He gripped my hand for a long moment. "Be well, kiddo."

Matt and I strolled across the dew-heavy lawn. I had lost my sandals somewhere, and Penny's flip flops offered no defense against the cold droplets. I didn't care. I wanted to feel every one of them. Neither of us spoke. We stepped aboard, and Matt wiped the dew off the seat in the stern. He brought pillows from the cuddly cabin and a sleeping bag. "Let's make you comfortable." He spread the warm flannel bag over our laps and plumped a pillow for my back, but the medication was wearing off and my back hurt like holy heck, so I leaned against him instead and rested my head on his shoulder.

The Milky Way suspended itself in icy splendor. Matt named the stars in the big dipper, then traced the snaky outline of Draco between the two dippers.

But there was something I had to know. "Who shot him, Matt?"

"Jake or I. One of us. Or both of us. I don't know."

"Is that one of your ghosts?"

"Absolutely. I've never killed anyone, and I've always hoped I wouldn't."

"Both you and Jake fired?"

"Yup. They'll analyze the bullets, of course, and we'll find out. If it turns out my shot killed him, then I have to be okay with that." He kissed the top of my head where the hair was gone. "I might even be glad. I never thought I'd hear myself say that. But it was you and Jordan and Bear or him." After a pause, he said. "I'd do it again in a heartbeat."

"I can't believe some of the things I've said to you,

and you never hit back. You just let me rant on."

He interlaced our fingers. "You didn't know."

"This is a DEA case, but Mary thinks you work for the FBI. Is that true?"

"Even my mother doesn't know who signs my paychecks." Matt pointed out how much the big dipper had rotated since we'd first looked at it. Then he said, "I think we need a little refreshment. Are you interested in red wine and chocolate sandwich cookies with chocolate filling? It's my favorite snack."

"Mine, too."

"Not really."

"Honest."

He chuckled.

"You already know that." I grinned at him. "But I can't drink wine until my liver heals."

"It's a nice round Merlot with berry flavors and a hint of chocolate. We'll let it age until you're better."

He kissed me, softly at first, and then more deeply, urgently.

I felt as if I was falling into his soul. "I want to know what that kiss means."

"Soon," he said. He trailed a finger, light as butterfly wings, across my lips. "I want to know, too. Not tonight, but soon."

His answer puzzled me, but my head was spinning, and I didn't have the energy to pursue it. I would soon, I decided. We drank lemonade out of plastic champagne glasses Matt found somewhere down in the cuddly cabin.

With a note of pride, he pointed out that the cookies were home-made, fresh and crisp. They tasted like heaven, better than any I'd ever eaten, but I bit my swollen cheek when I tried to chew, so I gave the rest of mine to him.

The alarm on his watch buzzed. The pink light of dawn arrived in the east as he punched in numbers on his phone. "Did we do it?" he asked. He listened, spoke a few words, listened again. Watching his face, I saw the tension lines around his eyes relax. Then he broke into a grin and hung up. "Yes!" He pumped his arm above his head. "We did it. We got them all—all the ones we know, that is. Man, that makes me feel better."

"Me, too."

He put his fingers under my chin. "You had to face the worst one alone, all by yourself." He looked at me in the pale light. "I'll never forgive myself for that."

I shook my head. Gently, I pushed his hand away. I opened my mouth to say I forgave him, but it was still too fresh. I wanted to go back a couple of minutes, before he mentioned Devine, but I couldn't, so instead I said, "Alicia's medicine is wearing off. My back feels like I've got the worst sunburn a person could possibly have. The back of my head is even worse."

He brought me some water. In the pocket of Penny's sweat pants, I found the pills from Alicia.

"Let me spray it with sunburn stuff." He searched the cabin and came back shaking a can. "This will make it numb for a while."

I heard the hiss of the spray and felt the mist on my naked head, then lifted my shirt so he could cover my back. It felt so cold I shivered, and then the pain slowly started to ease.

"Want to shock everybody and stay out the rest of the night?" he asked. "We could get inside sleeping bags down below."

"Jordy's going to tell everybody I drove around the lake with no clothes on. You think they'll be shocked if I don't come in?"

Laughing softly, he bent to go into the cabin, then looked back over his shoulder. "No expectations, honest."

Biting my lip, I nodded. I wasn't sure, but I thought "expectations" might be just what the doctor ordered, not yet, but soon.

Matt spread a sleeping bag over the upholstered foam mattress, flannel side up. Then he pulled the one he'd put around our legs over it and zipped them together.

The bed occupied the whole V berth, so I sat on the very edge, as much out of the way as possible. In the faint reddish light of the gas pump sign on the dock, I watched the contours of his body, on his hands and knees, making a soft, safe place for us. As he backed off the bed, he lifted the top bag. "In you go."

Plumping a pillow, he nestled it under my head, then climbed in beside me. With our feet in the narrow end of the berth, and our heads together on the pillow, we saw the fading stars through the open companionway. Like kids in a tree house, we counted them before they winked out for another day. In spite of the medication and sunburn spray, the back of my head hurt, so I rolled onto my side. Matt put his arm around me, inviting me to rest on his shoulder.

Once we were settled, he said, "I never thought I'd get to meet you. One night, I came to the theater all pumped to go backstage and talk to you after the performance. I decided I'd just go find out if you'd consider walking down the street with me for a glass of wine." He ran his hand lightly down my arm.

"But?"

"I chickened out. I got as far as the corridor to the dressing rooms, you know, with the old brick wall on one side, and didn't know whether to turn right or left. My heart was skipping beats and my hands got sweaty, so I left."

"You? Tough lawman that you are? Seriously, I can't imagine that."

He laughed, a soft happy chortle. "Yup. Bad guys I can handle: con men, thieves, kidnappers, but you women are so awesome you scare me."

I rested my hand on his chest and he folded his hand over mine. I couldn't remember when I'd felt so warm and safe. In spite of my fears for Bear, my eyes closed. For a moment I thought I could get used to going to bed this way. Then I was suddenly wide awake again. *Heather, what on earth are you thinking about?*

I stared out a porthole at the dawn. Matt made his living doing very dangerous things. He lied about where he was going and what he was doing, lied for a good reason, but all the same. What if he didn't come back one night? I thought about how hard it had been to say goodbye to my sister, Harmony, and how I still woke up some mornings and expected her to be there.

Matt's breathing had slowed and the rhythmic rise and fall of his chest deepened. His heartbeat, strong and steady under my palm, calmed me. In the stillness of the morning, the boat lay quietly at dock. There was no lapping of waves against the hull, no rocking. The vet had not called, so Bear had made it through the night.

I'd deal with my feelings about Matt tomorrow. I couldn't keep my eyes open any longer.

****

My dreams did not disturb me. Grandma Garnet stood on pointe, holding a sparkling, many-colored wand. Her feet, in tiny white satin ballet slippers, moved so quickly I could hardly see them. She jumped into the air and stayed suspended above me, her sequined tutu stiffly extended around her hips. She waved her wand. "*Voilà*! Your name is Katherina. You are the star of *Taming*." Swooping gracefully around me in a full circle, she landed with a little thump on the floor. Her wand floated toward me and hung in front of my face, rotating and sending off showers of scintillating, multicolored sparks. "Try it. My wand is quite magical." Smiling, she did a pirouette. "It will give you whatever you want."

I reached for the wand, but it moved away.

She pushed it back toward me. "Go ahead. Why not have this handsome young man?"

She seemed so real, I spoke her name. She started to fade. I opened my eyes to the bright light of morning.

Chapter Twenty-Two

Ten days later, Mary got up from her lounge chair as I squeaked open the screen door and came out onto the deck. She waved her romance novel toward the parking space at the side of the cabin. "Bear's looking like his old self this morning. He's helping the boys."

Dropping my duffel bag on the deck, I looked over the railing. While Jordan rinsed suds off my car with the hose, Travis stood to one side of the graveled area, holding a dripping car wash mitt in one hand and my dog's collar in the other, making sure the dressing that crisscrossed his chest stayed dry. I hurried down the stairs. "You two are wonderful!"

Travis gave me a half-smile. "Bogey's all clean and shiny."

Jordan bent to turn the water off. "Yeah, we didn't think Bear should have to ride in a dusty car." He grinned, and mischief danced in his eyes.

Mary laughed. "You are a rotten child."

The four of us pushed and pulled until the canvas top folded down into a tidy ridge. Travis carried my bag down from the deck. Biceps bunching, he lifted it over Bogey's side to put it on the back seat. "Thanks, you guys," I said. "I'm going to miss you."

Jordan grinned. "Well, what about us? We won't have Bear." He tipped his head to one side and looked at his mother. "Just joking, Mom. Honest, Heather, we'll miss you too, won't we, Trav?" I rumpled his damp red hair and he ducked away. "It'll just be an ordinary summer when you're gone."

I hugged Mary. "There's no way to thank you. I wouldn't have made it without you."

Her arms tightened around me. "Promise you'll come back before summer's over." Her voice quavered. She patted my shoulder as we stepped apart.

"Bring Bear," Jordan and Travis chorused.

"As if I would dare come without him." I took a last look at the lake, gleaming like hammered pewter under the overcast sky, then motioned Bear into the car. Gingerly, he climbed up, walked across the driver's seat, and settled on the passenger side. I brushed his paw prints off and got in.

Jordan swung the door shut with just the right amount of force to make it latch on the first try. The engine started immediately. I patted the dash. "Bogey may be ancient, but I can always count on him." I eased the clutch out and turned up toward the service road. Jordy stood with his arm around his mother's waist and with his other hand, held two fingers above Travis' head. Mary and Travis waved. For a moment, they were all framed in the rear-view mirror, and then they disappeared as I turned toward Sam's house. Everything blurred, and I had to grab a tissue.

Bogey tackled the steep hill leading to the highway without hesitation. I reached over and grabbed a handful of hair on the back of Bear's neck. "It's good to be heading home, huh?" His eyes narrowed to slits as the wind blew in his face. Just like a man, he said nothing.

The cloud cover kept me from roasting as I drove

south along the Columbia River. The wind blowing through my little fringe of hair reminded me that I was able, at last, to do what I wanted to do, and I knew exactly what that was. Alex had phoned two days before to tell me that during rehearsals, Victoria had stormed out of the theater, screaming at the director because he said she was lisping. Alex thought she was on her way to San Francisco. If he was right, then I'd play Katherina in *Taming of the Shrew* after all.

"We'll be spending a lot of time together," he said. "I hope you'll be comfortable being on stage with me."

"I haven't forgotten that you dumped me for Victoria."

"I was a fool," he said. "We probably need to talk about that."

"Maybe."

Regardless of our relationship, working with an actor of his caliber had been my dream ever since high school drama camp. I felt giddy every time I thought about it. In fact, sometimes, like when I told Mary, my grin was just as silly as Bear's. Actually, at times I laughed simply because I was happy to be alive, that Jordy was alive, and Bear. These were gifts for which I thanked all the good in the universe every day.

At Wenatchee, I turned away from the river onto Highway 2 West. I pushed a country western CD into the player, cranked up the volume and warbled along with Patsy Cline. In no time, I breezed through Leavenworth. The clouds hung low and dense over the canyon as I started up Stevens Pass, but still no rain fell. Just as well. I wasn't stopping to put the top up.

I thought how glad I'd be to see Grandma Garnet at her brick Tudor on Lake Washington and share a pot of tea. I couldn't wait to tell her about my dream of her in her sequined tutu, and her magic wand, and how it had come true, at least the part about the role of Katherina. I wasn't so sure about the rest of it. Why not have this handsome young man indeed.

At the summit, the clouds thinned out and I saw clear blue sky ahead, a total reversal of the usual weather pattern. Mary would've said it was an omen, of something good, I'd have guessed.

My phone rang. I fished it out of the waste basket on the transmission hump and touched the green button. It had to be Janice, full of news from the theater. But it wasn't.

"Hi, beautiful."

I steered to the shoulder and stopped at the side of the road across from the ski lodge.

"I called Mary's cabin and she said you'd left." Matt sounded excited. Where are you?"

I grinned. "On top of the mountain."

"I want to make reservations for dinner at Ray's Boat House, get a table on the deck, so we can celebrate and watch the sunset. Would you enjoy that?"

A picture of the highway winding through the little towns on the way to Seattle popped into my head. It was a slow road. It could take forever to get there. I put Bogey in gear and started down the mountain.

A word about the author...

I have studied writing in Paris and Seattle, and I write the galley column for *Pacific Yachting* magazine. *Murder Unrehearsed* is my first novel.

I am a physical therapist, a foodie, a fanatic about good chocolate, and a private pilot. I lived aboard an old wood motor yacht for seventeen years, and in my dreams, I'm a famous author, a pianist of renown, an acceptable watercolor artist, and a globe-trotting yogini.

I'd love to hear from you. Please visit me at:

http://roxannedunn.com